4 75

W9-BJJ-120

"I think you're making a fool of me..."

"No!"

"Yes." Isobel put her key in the door. "Stop pretending. I know you're not interested in me. Men like you—well, men of your... background," she amended awkwardly, "do not get involved with frumpish spinsters with attitude. I'm sure you think it's amusing to play these games, but I know there's something more to it than that."

"That's not true."

"What's not true?"

"That—that you're a frumpish spinster," Patrick told her impatiently. "What do you want me to say? That you're a very sexy lady? That any man would be proud to think you were interested in him?"

"I don't want you to say anything," she exploded hotly, sure now that he was just playing a game. "Go away, Mr. Riker. I'm not interested. Not in you, not in your proposition and certainly not in your lies!"

ANNE MATHER began writing when she was a child, progressing through torrid teenage romance novels to the kind of adult romance fiction she likes to read now. She's married, and lives in the north of England. After writing, she enjoys reading, driving and traveling to different places to find settings for new novels. She considers herself very lucky to do something that she not only enjoys but also gets paid for.

Books by Anne Mather

HARLEQUIN PRESENTS
1697—STRANGE INTIMACY
1722—BRITTLE BONDAGE
1731—RAW SILK
1759—TREACHEROUS LONGINGS
1797—A WOMAN OF PASSION
1845—RELATIVE SINS

Don't miss any of our special offers. Write to us at the following address for information on our newest releases.

Harlequin Reader Service
U.S.: 3010 Walden Ave., P.O. Box 1325, Buffalo, NY 14269
Canadian: P.O. Box 609, Fort Erie, Ont. L2A 5X3

Anne Mather

Wicked Caprice

Harlequin Books

TORONTO • NEW YORK • LONDON
AMSTERDAM • PARIS • SYDNEY • HAMBURG
STOCKHOLM • ATHENS • TOKYO • MILAN
MADRID • WARSAW • BUDAPEST • AUCKLAND

If you purchased this book without a cover you should be aware that this book is stolen property. It was reported as "unsold and destroyed" to the publisher, and neither the author nor the publisher has received any payment for this "stripped book."

ISBN 0-373-11869-4

WICKED CAPRICE

First North American Publication 1997.

Copyright © 1996 by Anne Mather.

All rights reserved. Except for use in any review, the reproduction or utilization of this work in whole or in part in any form by any electronic, mechanical or other means, now known or hereafter invented, including xerography, photocopying and recording, or in any information storage or retrieval system, is forbidden without the written permission of the publisher, Harlequin Enterprises Limited, 225 Duncan Mill Road, Don Mills, Ontario, Canada M3B 3K9.

All characters in this book have no existence outside the imagination of the author and have no relation whatsoever to anyone bearing the same name or names. They are not even distantly inspired by any individual known or unknown to the author, and all incidents are pure invention.

This edition published by arrangement with Harlequin Books S.A.

® and TM are trademarks of the publisher. Trademarks indicated with ® are registered in the United States Patent and Trademark Office, the Canadian Trade Marks Office and in other countries.

Printed in U.S.A.

CHAPTER ONE

SHE didn't look like the kind of woman he had expected.

Jillian's description of her had been fairly explicit, and it was hard to match up her portrayal of a vicious, self-seeking seductress with the slim, pale creature facing him across the counter.

'Can I help you?'

Her voice was attractive, certainly, low and slightly throaty, and probably inclined to a breathless huskiness when her sexual needs were being met. Was she the kind of woman who just moaned her pleasure, or did she whisper erotic words of approval in Richard's ear? Either way, it was hard to imagine his brother-in-law being interested in such a colourless female. In the past, his tastes had run in an entirely different direction.

'Hmm...? Oh, yes.'

Patrick glanced quickly about him, realising that apart from himself the shop was empty. He had spent so long studying her appearance that the other customers had all been dealt with, and her question caught him unawares, his mind empty of the reason why he'd purportedly come into the shop.

'Shells,' he said hastily as the excuse he'd adopted to enter the establishment popped back into his mind. He'd seen a necklace of shells in the window and it had seemed a suitable item to select.

'Shells?' she echoed pleasantly. 'You're a collector of shells? Do you mean shells that have just been polished and are otherwise in their natural state? Or perhaps you like these abstract collages? They've proved very popular, actually.'

The square frame she had selected from the display behind the counter made Patrick cringe. The childish daubings of

paint on shells, whose haphazard arrangement on a wooden
backing looked more abstracted than abstract, appalled him,
and he couldn't imagine anyone finding its composition
attractive.

'Um . . . it was a necklace, actually,' he said, casting a
doubtful glance over his shoulder. 'In the window. I thought
it might suit my niece.'

Though he could never give it to her, he reflected ruefully. He could picture Jillian's outrage if he turned up with
a necklace bought from *that woman's* shop. No matter that
Susie might like it. Even considering doing such a thing
would constitute a betrayal of the highest order in his sister's eyes. Besides, there was always the possibility that
Richard might recognise it, and Jillian would prefer her
husband not to know she'd interfered.

'Oh, yes. I know the one.'

With a smile, she came out from behind the counter and
crossed the sales area to approach the window he'd indicated. As she passed, Patrick was assailed by the delicate
aroma of her perfume, an odour that mingled what he
thought might be lily of the valley and rosewater with the
feminine warmth of her body.

He was also made aware of the fact that she moved with
a distinctive grace for such a tall young woman, her hips
swaying rhythmically as she strode across the floor, her full
skirt swishing softly about her ankles. Her hair was plaited,
a thick, glossy, toffee-coloured braid that bobbed about
between her shoulderblades. It was almost the exact same
colour as her eyes, he mused reluctantly, though her brows
were darker, her lashes thick and straight.

She was also wearing boots, he saw as she bent to remove
the necklace from the window—thick-soled boots, which
Patrick would have considered more suitable for going
hiking. Or perhaps mountaineering, he amended drily.
Whatever else Richard had seen in her, he couldn't have
been attracted by the way she dressed.

'Here we are,' she said, straightening, and Patrick dragged
his eyes away from the provocative cleft that had been revealed when she'd bent over. For all his dismissal of her

charms, he had to admit there was something about her. Despite the shapeless clothes, she did possess a sensuality that wasn't immediately apparent.

'Thanks.'

He took the necklace from her, and was surprised by the jolt of awareness he felt when her slim hand brushed his. Concentrating his attention on the necklace, he couldn't help wondering if she'd felt it too, though when he permitted himself a quick glance through his lashes she appeared to be as cool and composed as before.

'It's the last one,' she said, and for a moment he couldn't for the hell of him think what she was talking about.

'The last...?'

'Yes, the last necklace,' she clarified smoothly. 'I think people have mostly bought them for children. As you can see, the string isn't very long.'

'Yes.'

Patrick felt curiously perplexed. He was used to being in control of most situations, but for a moment there he had felt at a distinct disadvantage. It was the unfamiliarity of his surroundings, he told himself, and of this young woman, who seemed to bear little resemblance to the promiscuous hussy his sister had described. She could be everything Jillian had accused her of being—God knew, appearances were often deceptive—but had Richard succumbed to her wiles, or had she succumbed to his?

'Do you like it?'

Once again, her question aroused a most unsuitable response inside him, and he felt a faintly amused impatience with himself for allowing his instincts to govern his head. For God's sake, the woman wasn't even pretty, and in those clothes she wouldn't attract a second glance. Yet, for some strange reason, he was aware of her, in a way he hadn't been aware of a woman for years.

If ever..

'It's pretty,' he said now, the word springing obviously to mind, and she nodded in agreement.

'I think so,' she agreed. 'These fan-shaped shells are so delicate. I love that shade of pink. It would be impossible to produce it artificially.'

'Mmm.'

Patrick was noncommittal, aware that by admiring the necklace he was making it doubly hard to reject it later. After all, he hadn't come here to admire the merchandise; he was supposed to be finding out what she wanted from Richard. In Jillian's opinion, she had to have a price. Richard's women always did.

'You don't like it?'

His doubts, albeit of a different nature, had communicated themselves to her, and she tilted her head to look up at him. Immediately, he was aware of the purity of her profile, of the cheekbones that gave her face such a good basic structure, and the mouth, which had parted slightly in enquiry.

He wanted to taste that mouth, he realised in a horrifying revelation. He wanted to crush it, and shape it with his tongue, and suck the full lower lip into his mouth. He wanted to see if she tasted as good as she smelled, and if that delicate pink tongue, presently trapped between two rows of white teeth, was as moist and juicy as it appeared...

He drew a steadying breath. For God's sake, he chided himself as his trousers felt uncomfortably tight all of a sudden. What the hell was the matter with him? He hadn't realised he was so desperately in need of sex.

Assuming an interest in a colourful display of quilts, he succeeded in putting some space between them. 'It's not that,' he said, realising he hadn't answered her question. 'I just don't know if Susie...if she would like it.'

'Susie?' She'd latched onto the word, and he cursed himself for using his niece's name so thoughtlessly. 'A colleague of mine's daughter is called Susie too. It's a nice name, isn't it? Is it short for Susannah?'

'No.' It was, but he wasn't going to admit it. 'Um...it's just Susie, actually. Not an abbreviation. Her...parents chose it. Her grandmother's name is the same.'

'I see.'

He wondered if she did. He hoped not. Nevertheless, he had gone over the top with the explanations, and if he'd regretted using Susie's name before he felt doubly impatient with himself now.

Something had to be done to divert the conversation, and, smoothing the fabric of one of the quilts between his thumb and forefinger, he cast what he hoped was a casual glance over his shoulder. 'Is this what you call patchwork?'

'That's right.' His enquiry had achieved what he least wanted; it had brought her after him, and he was intensely aware of her now, hovering at his elbow. 'Actually, they're made by an old lady who's almost crippled with arthritis. But her needlework is exquisite, don't you agree?'

As Patrick had no idea what was required to make one of the padded spreads, he merely nodded his approval, and moved on to a table piled with soft toys. At least here he could be more knowledgeable; the stuffed menagerie was obviously attractive, the prices mirroring the small-shop status, yet in no way diminishing the toys' appeal.

'They're handmade too,' she murmured as Patrick admired a pair of rabbits. 'In fact, everything we sell is handcrafted. We provide an outlet for people who wouldn't otherwise have anywhere to sell their goods.'

Jillian hadn't told him that. But then, why would she? She wasn't interested in the aims of the business, just in its proprietor... or was that proprietrix? Anyway, just because this young woman was doing her bit to help the independent producer it didn't make the situation any more acceptable. She might be regarded as a saint by her suppliers and still live an execrable private life.

'Has the shop been open long, Miss—Miss—?' He stopped, as if he didn't already know her name by rote.

'Herriot,' she inserted quickly. 'Isobel Herriot. And I opened the shop almost five years ago.' She paused. 'Why?'

'Just curious,' he answered smoothly, a smile erasing any suspicion. 'You've got quite a choice of items. I wondered how you managed to sustain your stock.'

'Oh...' She shrugged her slim shoulders, and against his will his eyes were drawn to her chest. For such a slim young woman she had rather full breasts, and the way they moved beneath the gauze shirt she was wearing made him wonder if she wore a bra. 'It was a struggle to begin with. But we're getting there now, I think.'

So was he, thought Patrick irritably, wishing he had never agreed to come here. Dammit, the girl was screwing his brother-in-law, and he was acting as if that circumstance turned him on. It didn't. He despised Richard and he despised her for putting his sister's marriage in jeopardy. Not to mention risking their children's happiness. Ten-year-old Susie and her brother Nigel, who was six, didn't deserve to be treated as if their lives were of no account.

His eyes hardened. 'Do you own the shop, Miss Herriot?' he enquired, keeping his tone neutral, and she gave a rueful sigh.

'In such a prime position?' She grimaced. 'Chance would be a fine thing. No, my new landlord is the colleague I was telling you about. The one who has a daughter called Susie—Susannah.'

'Ah.'

Patrick acted as if he didn't already know that Shannon Holdings had recently acquired the lease on the row of small businesses that fronted this side of the high street in Horsham-on-the-Water. Situated almost midway between Stratford-on-Avon and Stow-on-the-Wold, the little Cotswold village of Horsham attracted a lot of passing trade. But it was also true that many people came to Horsham for its own sake, visiting the old Norman church, and the monastery, where a delicious foaming mead had been made for more years than anyone could remember.

'Of course,' she went on, almost absently, 'there's going to be an increase in the rents. Old Mrs Foxworth, who used to own the Foxworth estate, let the tenants rent these properties for a pittance, so long as the buildings were kept in good repair. It was a kind of *noblesse oblige*, I suppose, and we'd all begun to think it would go on indefinitely. But the people who've bought the estate—some London company, I believe—obviously won't feel so charitable. How could they? They don't know us. Richard says he'll do his best to put our case forward, but we don't hold out much hope.'

Patrick endeavoured not to show his true feelings. 'Richard?' he echoed politely. He bit into the inner flesh of his lower lip. 'Your new landlord—I remember.'

'Well, he isn't exactly our new landlord,' she explained, and the faintly terse edge to her tone seemed to indicate that she had realised she was discussing private matters with a stranger. 'Rich—Mr Gregory, that is—is just an employee of the company.' Her nostrils flared in sudden impatience. 'And I don't see what he or anyone else can do.'

Patrick found himself resenting the way Richard had represented himself to her, but that was the least of his troubles. How well did she know his brother-in-law? And what exactly had Richard promised to do?

Choosing his words with care, Patrick laid the shell necklace on the counter. 'You sound as if you have a champion, at least,' he remarked guardedly. 'Have you known this Mr—ah—Gregory long?'

'Not long.' Her tone was clipped now, and he was very much afraid he'd overplayed his hand. She lifted the necklace, cradling it in fingers that were long and vaguely artistic. 'Have you made a decision?'

Patrick blinked. 'Oh—about the necklace,' he said, aware that she was looking at him a little warily now. 'Um—yes. Yes, I'll have it.' He examined the price tag and pulled out his wallet. 'Perhaps you could wrap it for me. I'll be back this way in a couple of days and I'll collect it then.'

'I can wrap it now,' she said, and he was racking his brains for a suitable excuse for her not to do so when a group of elderly American tourists entered the shop.

'Thursday,' he said, throwing a couple of notes onto the counter. 'I can see you're going to be busy, and I can wait.'

With the door closed behind him, Patrick breathed a little easier, though why he should imagine that by returning to the shop two days hence he might learn any more about her relationship with Richard he didn't know. He could hardly come right out and ask her, even if that was what Jillian would have him do. But then, Jillian wanted him to

threaten the girl with God knew what kind of retribution
if she continued to have an affair with her husband, and
she was aware of the kind of leverage he could bring to
bear if Isobel Herriot refused to do as he said.

His car was parked further along the high street, and,
opening the rear door, Patrick slid into the back of the
Bentley with some relief. 'Let's go, Joe,' he said, when the
impassive Muzambe turned to give him a questioning
glance. 'Portland Street first, and then home.'

Joe Muzambe put the big car into gear, switched on the
indicator, and pulled out into a gap in the stream of traffic
passing through the village. 'You don't want to stop at Mrs
Gregory's?' he asked, with the familiarity of long service,
and Patrick, dragging a file of papers from his briefcase,
gave him a retiring look.

'No, I do not,' he replied, aware that the chauffeur was
referring to the fact that they'd pass within a couple of
miles of Jillian's house on their way back to town. 'I don't
have anything to tell her,' he added, with an irritation that
was directed as much at himself as at his sister. 'Now, if
you don't mind, can we get going? I want to do some work.'

CHAPTER TWO

'BUT who was he?'

Christine Nelson perched on the edge of the counter and regarded her friend and employer with impatient eyes. There were times when Isobel's other-worldliness really bugged her, and her lack of interest in the dishy male Christine had seen coming out of the craft shop was positively infuriating.

'I've told you, I don't know,' replied Isobel, examining the figures in the cash book which she was trying to balance with the contents of the till. 'He didn't say, and I could hardly ask him. It's not as if it matters, after all.'

'Of course it matters.' Christine was frustrated. 'Do you want to live in this old backwater all your life? For heaven's sake, you should have seen the car he got into. If it wasn't a Rolls-Royce, I'll—'

'Chris, please!'

Isobel was finding it increasingly difficult to concentrate with her young assistant prattling on about a man they were unlikely to see again. For all he'd paid for the necklace, and for all he'd said he'd be back, Isobel was chary. She had the feeling he'd been looking for something she didn't sell.

But what?

'Well...' Christine wasn't daunted '...it's time you realised you're not getting any younger. The old body clock is ticking, Issy. And you are almost thirty. I wouldn't be so blasé, if I were you.'

'But you're not me, are you?' retorted Isobel, stung into her own defence. 'And I'm not a seventeen-year-old girl who still believes in fairy stories. If he is as—as good-looking as you think, and rich enough to drive a Rolls-Royce, he's not going to be interested in me, is he—an ageing spinster, with a mid-life crisis?'

'Now you're exaggerating,' declared Christine, getting down from the counter and scuffing her toe against the worn vinyl flooring. 'Just because I mentioned your age doesn't mean I think you're middle-aged. But you have to admit you're not getting any younger, and, knowing how you dote on those children of your brother's, I'd have thought you'd like a baby of your own.'

Isobel pressed her lips together. She was tempted to make some scathing retort, but she knew that anything she said could be misconstrued as sour grapes. Nevertheless, she resented Christine's assumption that all women must necessarily want to get married. She wasn't at all sure that that was an option she wanted to consider. She was quite happy being her own mistress, and although she didn't dislike men she'd never felt the slightest inclination to submit her will to that of some nebulous male.

Until today...

But that was ridiculous, and she knew it. As she secured the roll of notes with an elastic band and added them to the jingling coins already in the leather bag she used to carry the money to and from the bank, she acknowledged that Christine would have a field-day if she knew what her employer was really thinking. Because, far from being able to dismiss the attractive stranger from her mind, Isobel had hardly known a moment's peace since he had departed. To say that he had disturbed her was a vast understatement; it would be more accurate to compare an earthquake to the minor tremors they had felt in Wales.

'You would like to get married, wouldn't you?' Christine persisted, and Isobel wondered how they'd ever got onto this topic. A schoolfriend of Christine's had recently found herself pregnant and was having to get married, and since then Chris had become decidedly broody. Her own parents had produced seven children, and, since she was the daughter of a local farmer, she was well-versed in animal husbandry.

'I don't know,' Isobel answered now, collecting her cardigan from the room at the back of the shop. 'If you're finished, can we get going? I want to go to Stoddart's before they close.'

Christine had no choice but to precede her employer out of the shop, and Isobel set the alarm and then joined her. As she locked the door she couldn't help casting a faintly apprehensive look about her. But there was no sign of her intriguing visitor, or the expensive car that Christine had said he drove.

Leaving the younger girl to go her own way, Isobel went to the bank first, stowing the day's takings in the night safe before turning back to the local supermarket. She felt in need of some extra sustenance, and she put a bottle of white wine into her basket. At least she could afford to live reasonably comfortably, she reflected. Her grandmother's legacy had enabled her to do that.

But as she walked home, exchanging greetings with many of the other shopkeepers who were closing up for the night, she couldn't help wondering if that was why she hadn't got married before now. Being independent had its advantages, but it also made one more inclined to think things out. Her usual criterion, when some man began to show too close an interest in her, was to ask herself what she had to gain from the liaison. If the answer was nothing, as it invariably was, she ended the relationship. In consequence, she had remained detached from any emotional entanglements.

Her own parents were hardly a good example of married bliss. Although she was sure they cared about one another, they each lived their own lives. Her mother ran a fairly successful interior decorating business in Stratford, and her father was the local doctor, and therefore absorbed in his work. Isobel was their only daughter, but they had never put any pressure on her. She supposed they would appreciate a couple more grandchildren one day, but her brother's three seemed more than enough to be going on with.

Isobel's cottage was situated off the high street, in a narrow lane that backed onto the church. It was another of the advantages that her grandmother's legacy had given her. Until her grandmother died, she had been living and working in London.

Of course, she had been a part of the so-called rat race in those days. Leaving university with a double first in art and history, she had joined a well-known firm of auctioneers, with a view to becoming one of their in-house experts. The salary had been excellent and the work interesting, but the kind of social life she had been expected to enjoy had made her realise she was not really cut out for such political manoeuvring. She was basically a country girl who found life in the city rather shallow and specious. She was happiest with people who were not desperate to further their ambitions, and to whom an invitation to supper possessed no hidden agenda.

The crunch had come when her immediate superior had been dismissed because, according to her boss, she couldn't handle it. It had not been until Isobel, promoted in her place, had discovered what the 'it' was that he had been talking about that she had given in her notice. The fact that her grandmother had just died had seemed just an unhappy coincidence until the solicitor had informed her of the legacy the old lady had left her. With it she had been able to buy the cottage, and take her time looking around for an alternative occupation.

The idea of opening the craft shop had been an inspiration, and it had been amazing how quickly the advertisement she had placed in the local newspaper had borne fruit. Until then, the many amateur craftsmen and women in the area had not had a shop window in which to display their wares. They'd been obliged to offer their work at fairs and jumble sales, often accepting less than the articles were worth to obtain a sale. With the opening of Caprice, they had their opportunity, and Isobel was always amazed at how the standard of the merchandise she was offered just went up and up.

The past five years had been the happiest of her life, and it was only the vague apprehension she was feeling about the coming increase in the rent for the shop that was looming like a cloud on the horizon now. It depended how much it was, of course, but it wouldn't be easy absorbing the increase without putting up the cost of the goods she sold,

and while she had great faith in the quality of the work-
manship people often wanted designer names these days.

Still, she reflected, opening her front door and stepping
into the cool, scented shadows of her hallway, Richard had
promised to do his best to limit the increase. If he could
persuade his employers not to be too greedy, he would, and
the shopkeepers had little choice but to wait and trust his
judgement.

Once again, an old lady's death was proving decisive in
determining the direction that her life was going to take.
Old Mrs Foxworth, whose estate had once encompassed all
the land and property in and around Horsham, had died
a little over a year ago, and since then the majority of the
estate's remaining assets had been sold to Shannon
Holdings. A public company, with dealings in many of the
developed countries of the world, it was a world away from
Mrs Foxworth's agent, with whom they had had an almost
intimate association. Barney Penlaw was retired now—
compulsorily, some people said—and in his place they had
Richard Gregory, who, for all his smiles and old-world
courtesy, was still the face of capitalism, she supposed.

When he'd first appeared, about three months ago,
Christine had made the same comments about him as she
had made about the man who'd bought the shell necklace,
and in Richard's case Isobel had to admit they were not so
misplaced. He had made no secret of the fact that he was
attracted to her, and although she hadn't encouraged him
she knew his frequent visits to Horsham were not just to
report on the expected increase in the rents.

But Isobel remained indifferent to his overtures. He was
married, for one thing, and although he maintained that
he and his wife were having problems the very fact that
there were children proved that this hadn't always been the
case. Besides, she had no wish to get involved with him and
possibly jeopardise the rights of her fellow shopkeepers,
should their relationship come to grief. She liked Richard:
he made her laugh. But she had yet to find a man who
satisfied all her needs. Sometimes she thought she
never would.

It was a warm evening. June had been a rather wet month so far, but for the past couple of days the weather had improved, and Isobel couldn't wait to get the cottage windows open. In spite of the pot-pourri she'd brought from the shop and kept in dishes about the cottage to keep the air sweet and flowery, the heat had made the atmosphere a little musty, and dust motes danced in the shafts of sunlight that swept through an opened blind.

But, for all that, the cottage still charmed her in much the same way as it had always done. Perhaps it was because it was hers, her first real home of her own. The flat she had shared with two other girls in London had never been that, and returning to live with her parents would have created difficulties she could see more clearly in retrospect.

In any event, she had been glad not to have to test that relationship, and in the five years since she'd moved in she had made many small improvements. Not least the installation of an adequate heating system, she reflected wryly. The first winter at Lime Cottage, she'd shivered in her bed.

But now the cottage welcomed her, its oak beams and funny inglenook fireplace gaining in character now that its shortcomings had been dealt with. It wasn't big, just a living room and breakfast room-cum-kitchen downstairs, and two bedrooms—one of which was little more than a boxroom—and a bathroom upstairs. She'd added an Aga and a shower, and both the kitchen and bathroom had needed modernising, of course. But she had retained the cottage's harmony, and visitors always remarked on its feeling of warmth.

Isobel put the things she had bought on the kitchen table, unloading perishable items into the fridge before going upstairs to change and take a shower. It was one of her idiosyncrasies that she liked to bathe and change her clothes before sitting down to supper. Then she could look forward to a pleasant evening ahead, with good food, a glass of wine, and possibly some music on the radio.

She had a television, but she seldom watched it, preferring the radio or her own choice of music on compact disc. She wasn't particularly highbrow in her choice of listening: she enjoyed a lot of modern music, particularly jazz. But her favourite composer had to be Chopin, his sonatas filling the cottage with beauty whenever she felt depressed.

Because it was a warm evening, she didn't bother getting dressed again, but came downstairs wearing a dark red silk kimono with orchids appliquéd along the satin lapels. It was hardly her sort of thing, but her mother had brought it back from a buying trip to Tokyo, and although the colour was more vivid than she was used to there was no doubt that it was superbly comfortable to wear.

She was stir-frying some vegetables to go with the omelette she intended to have for her supper when someone knocked at the door.

She wasn't expecting anyone, and although it wasn't late she had hoped to spend the evening alone. Neither of her parents was likely to call without prior warning, and there'd been no messages on her answering machine from either them or her brother and sister-in-law.

For a heart-stopping moment, she thought of the man who had come into the shop earlier. Was it possible he had decided he wanted to take the necklace tonight after all? But no. That was ludicrous. He didn't know where she lived, and in any case she never brought other people's purchases home.

Removing the pan from the heat, she wiped her hands on a paper towel and surveyed her appearance with some misgiving. She had washed her hair in the shower, and although she'd used the drier on it she'd left it loose about her shoulders, and her image now wasn't at all the one she preferred others to see.

The knocker was rapped again, and she heaved a sigh. With all the windows in the cottage open, she could hardly pretend she wasn't at home. No, there was nothing for it but to see who it was, and hope she could get rid of them. She grimaced. It might be the vicar, after all.

The idea of the fairly sanctimonious Mr Mason being confronted by the scarlet kimono made her smile, and she was attempting to straighten her expression as she opened the door. But it wasn't the Reverend Mason, it was Richard

Gregory, and he stared at her as if he'd never seen her before.

'Hello,' he said, his eyes darkening. 'You look nice. Are you going somewhere special?'

'In this?' Isobel was mildly sarcastic. 'I don't think so somehow.' She paused. 'How did you know where I live?'

'Oh, Chris told me ages ago,' responded Richard without hesitation. 'Can I come in?' He lifted his hand. 'I've brought a bottle of wine.'

Isobel's tongue circled her lips. 'It's very kind of you, but—'

'You're not going to turn me away, are you?' His face assumed a mournful expression. 'I've driven all the way from Oxford. I thought you'd be glad to see me.'

Isobel suppressed a sigh. 'Now why should you imagine that?' she asked, vaguely resenting his presumption. 'I'm sorry. I—I should have explained at once. I am going out this evening, actually. I was just getting ready.' She crossed the fingers of one hand behind her back, and gave him an apologetic smile. 'I'm afraid you've had a wasted journey.'

Richard's features suffused with a rather unbecoming colour. He was very fair, his hair so light that it appeared almost white sometimes, and the redness that entered his cheeks gave his face a hectic look. He was obviously disappointed, but there was something more than disappointment in his manner. If she hadn't known he was such a good-humoured man, she'd have said he was angry. There was something almost aggressive in his stance.

'And that's it?' he said, revealing a side of himself that hitherto she hadn't encountered, and Isobel felt a momentary twinge of fear. After all, the cottage was at least a dozen yards from its nearest neighbour, and the elderly couple whose property adjoined hers were away.

'I'm sorry,' she said again, and something—perhaps an awareness that he was in danger of destroying their friendly association—seemed to bring him to his senses.

'Yes,' he said, in an entirely different tone. 'Yes, I should have phoned first; I realise that now. Well—' he handed her the bottle '—there's no point in wasting this. Have it with my blessing, and I'll see you next week.'

Isobel wanted to refuse the wine. The way she was feeling at the moment, she wanted nothing of his to mar the peaceful ambience of the cottage. But it was easier to accept it than risk creating another confrontation, and she thanked him very politely as she bid him farewell.

It was only as she closed the door that she wondered if by chance he could have smelt the stir-fried vegetables. It seemed likely, which might account for his sudden aggressive mood. If he'd thought that she was lying to him, he could have felt resentful, but, either way, she was extremely glad he had gone.

CHAPTER THREE

'HE WENT to see her on Tuesday night. I know he did.'
Jillian's voice was filled with outrage. 'I thought you were
going to speak to her, Patrick. You promised me you would.'

Patrick expelled a resigned breath. 'How do you know
he went to see her?' he asked, avoiding a direct answer.
'Did you follow him?'

'Of course not.' Jillian sounded indignant now. 'But I
did check the milometer like you told me to, and there was
over a hundred miles more on Wednesday morning.'

Patrick cast the towel he had been using to dry himself
aside and bent closer to the mirror to examine his overnight
stubble. He had hardly got out of the shower when his
housekeeper had come to tell him that Mrs Gregory was
on the telephone. He'd half expected her to ring him last
night, but it had been fairly late when he'd got back from
Basle.

'Well?' Jillian was impatient. 'Did you speak to her or
didn't you? For heaven's sake, Pat, I'm getting desperate.
Rich has never been so indifferent to my feelings before.'

'Don't you mean he's never been so reckless before?'
suggested her brother drily, wishing he'd never agreed to
get involved in this. 'The very fact that you use the word
"before" proves it. How many times does he need to be
unfaithful to you before you come to your senses?'

Jillian sniffed. 'I love him, Pat. You know that. I know
he has his faults, but deep inside he loves me too.'

Patrick stifled a groan. In his opinion, Richard Gregory
didn't love anyone but himself. At present, he was en-
amoured of the rather colourless young woman Patrick had
visited on Tuesday afternoon, but Patrick had no doubt
that Isobel Herriot was just a passing fancy and that pretty
soon there'd be some other contender for his brother-in-

law's affections. It wasn't as if she was a raving beauty, or possessed any outstanding attribute that Patrick could see. She was simply a village shopkeeper, with a personal axe to grind.

Or at least that was what he'd told himself as Joe Muzambe had driven him back to town. His own unwelcome reactions to the woman he'd put down to a hormonal imbalance. He hadn't seen Joanna in over a week, due to this problem with Richard and pressure of work. What he needed was an evening with his girlfriend, and time to expunge his sexual frustration. What he didn't need was an aberrant attraction to Richard's mistress, who was simply not his type.

'Then why don't *you* speak to him about it?' he asked now, unaware that he was still avoiding answering her question until she repeated it. Then, 'Yes. Yes, I saw her. You don't have anything to worry about, believe me.'

Jillian's hesitation was expressive. 'What do you mean?' she asked at last, and Patrick took another restraining breath.

'I mean that I can't imagine what—if anything—Rich sees in her,' he declared at last. 'She's—insipid, Jill. A nonentity. I can only assume he's in the mood for dowdy spinsters these days.'

Jillian uttered a cry. 'Do you think that makes me feel any better?'

'It should.' Patrick was growing impatient. 'Believe me, Jill, if you can just close your eyes for another couple of weeks, it'll all be over.'

'No!'

'What do you mean, no?'

'I mean I can't close my eyes to what's going on right under my nose. You don't know Rich as I do, Pat. This time I think he's serious. He doesn't have any time for me; he doesn't have any time for the children. Susie's beginning to notice. Just last night she asked me why Daddy doesn't play games with them any more.'

Patrick closed his eyes. 'You're exaggerating.'

'I'm not.' Jillian sniffed again. 'Anyway, what did you say to her? Did you tell her Rich was married? That he has a family who depend on him?'

'I think she knows,' admitted Patrick unwillingly, recalling that she'd mentioned Susie's name. 'As far as speaking to her goes, I'm not sure that would be an advantage. You could exacerbate the situation, if you see what I mean.'

'I don't see what you mean!' exclaimed Jillian resentfully. 'And it's not as if you don't have any power. What you're really saying is that you don't want to help me. That as far as you're concerned she holds all the cards.'

'No.' Patrick's jaw clamped, and he knew an uncharacteristic urge to hang up on her. This wasn't his problem, he told himself grimly. God, why couldn't she have married someone else?

'Well . . .' Jillian was obviously making no effort to hide the fact that she was upset—and disappointed in him. 'I suppose I shall have to go and see her myself—'

'You can't do that.' Patrick spoke through his teeth. Then, with great reluctance, he went on, 'All right, all right, I'll go and see her again. But I'm not making any promises. I'll just put your point of view across and see what she says.'

'You won't put her out of the shop?'

Patrick gasped. 'Put her out of the shop?' he echoed. 'What the hell are you talking about?'

'Well, Shannon Holdings do own the leases on all those shops, don't they?' Jillian pointed out silkily. 'If she wasn't one of your tenants, Rich would have no excuse to go and see her.'

Patrick's jaw sagged. 'And you think that would stop him?'

Jillian gulped defensively. 'It might.'

'Forget it,' said Patrick harshly. 'Just leave it with me. As I say, I'll see what I can do.'

With the phone safely returned to its hook, Patrick turned angrily towards the handbasin. Groping for his razor, he avoided meeting his eyes as he applied lather and scraped savagely at his beard. For God's sake, he thought frustratedly, Jillian was sometimes more trouble than all his overseas operations put together. Or, perhaps more accurately, Richard was. He wondered what she'd say if he suggested getting rid of his brother-in-law instead.

He knew he couldn't do it, of course. For all his faults, Richard was still family, and because, soon after he and Jillian had got married, he'd lost his position with a Japanese company due to their relocation to Taiwan Patrick had offered him the job.

It had been either that or suffer Jillian's recriminations. She had been pregnant with their first child at the time, and any idea of moving to the Far East had been out of the question so far as she was concerned. She'd wanted to stay in England; she'd wanted to keep her home and be near her family. It would have been a hard man indeed who could have withstood her pleas.

And, although Patrick was regarded in some quarters as a hard man, he had accommodated her. Since their father had died some years ago, he'd been regarded as the head of the family, and it was a responsibility he hadn't accepted lightly. Outside Shannon Holdings, it was the only responsibility he was prepared to shoulder. His ex-wife's greedy machinations had convinced him of that.

He cut his chin with the razor, the blood welling crimson over his jaw. Dammit he swore angrily, swabbing it with a towel and scowling at the stain on the pure white cotton, why couldn't Jillian solve her own problems? He had no desire to go back to Horsham, no desire to see Isobel Herriot again.

As luck would have it, he had a free morning. He hadn't been expected to arrive back from the conference in Switzerland until today, and although his managing director would expect to see him at this afternoon's meeting he had more than enough time to drive to Warwickshire and back again. All he had to do was pick up the phone and call Joe. In a little under an hour, he could be on his way.

Mrs Joyce had breakfast waiting for him, but apart from two cups of coffee and a slice of toast he barely touched it.

'Is something wrong?' asked Mrs Joyce fussily, knowing that he usually enjoyed her blueberry pancakes, and Patrick gave her an apologetic smile.

'I'm afraid I'm not hungry this morning, Mrs Joyce,' he said, folding his copy of the *Financial Times* and getting up from the table. 'Offer them to Joe when he gets here. I know he won't turn you down.'

'And have him suffering from indigestion all morning because he's had to hurry them?' Mrs Joyce rejoined tartly. 'If he's coming to pick you up, you know you'll be waiting. And Mr Muzambe is nothing if not conscientious.'

'Aren't you all?' murmured Patrick in an undertone, striking his thigh with the rolled-up newspaper as he walked out of the morning room. He didn't have time to massage Mrs Joyce's feelings. Right now he was fighting Jillian's battles, and he still had a business to run.

A couple of hours later, as they approached the turn-off for Banbury and Stratford, Patrick put away the papers he had been working on since they'd left London and applied his mind to the interview ahead. He grimaced. Not that it hadn't been on his mind ever since he'd spoken to Jillian, he admitted to himself irritably. His efforts to work on the journey were proof of that. He had read the last balance sheet at least half a dozen times.

'How much further?' he asked, more for something to say than anything else, and Joe Muzambe looked into the rear-view mirror and fixed him with a thoughtful look.

'Ten—twelve miles, maybe,' he answered, transferring his attention back to the road. 'Is this another fleeting visit, or will you be having lunch with the lady?'

Patrick scowled. 'How do you know it's a lady I'm going to see?'

'I heard,' replied Joe impassively, slowing for a round-about. 'Mrs Gregory isn't always fussy about keeping her voice down.'

'No.' Patrick conceded the point, aware that whatever was said between them would go no further. 'Let's hope I have some success this time. I don't want to make this journey again. I've got to go to the States on Monday, and I'm not going to have any more time.'

Joe bowed his bullet-shaped head. In common with a lot of young men of his age, he wore his head shaved, and that, combined with his broad shoulders and powerful physique, was enough to deter any would-be kidnapper. Patrick had had his share of threats, like any man in his position, and Joe served as both chauffeur and body-guard—and confidant, on occasion.

'Does that mean you won't be having lunch in Horsham?' Joe ventured, accelerating past a pair of cyclists, and Patrick gave him an impatient look.

'Yes, it does,' he said shortly, aware that Joe was bearing the brunt of his ill humour. 'Dammit, this isn't a social call.'

Joe shrugged, too used to his employer's moods to be put out. Besides, normally Patrick Shannon was an excellent employer, and it was only when his sister got on his back that other people suffered.

Meanwhile, Patrick was brooding over what to do about the shell necklace. All right, he had bought the damn thing, but he had never intended to return to collect it. OK, Isobel Herriot hadn't been what he had expected, and just for a few moments there she had briefly laid siege to his senses, but that was all it had been—a momentary aberration. The very idea of him and his brother-in-law sharing the same taste in women was ludicrous—apart from the very real emotions Jillian would feel if he told her he had been attracted to the woman too.

There wasn't a space to park in the high street this morning, so Patrick had Joe drop him off near the craft shop, and arranged to meet him outside the shop in fifteen minutes.

'In the car?' asked Joe, pushing his luck, and Patrick's eyes narrowed.

'In the car,' he agreed, stepping out onto the pavement. 'If you can find somewhere to park, get yourself a cup of coffee, right?'

'Right, boss,' agreed Joe sardonically, and Patrick's lips twitched at his attempt at humour. Bloody hell, he thought irritably, this was an impossible situation. He should have spoken to Richard first, not his mistress.

The trouble was that speaking to Richard was a little like trying to catch raindrops in your hands. Just when you thought you'd caught one, it slipped away through your fingers. Patrick had spoken to Richard before, and his brother-in-law had made promises he'd never had any intention of keeping. He knew that so long as Jillian wanted him Patrick didn't stand a chance.

Caprice.

As he'd done on that other occasion, Patrick looked in the shop window before venturing inside. Apart from a child and its mother, who appeared to be talking to someone behind the counter, the shop was empty.

Oh, well, he thought, he didn't have time to wait any longer. When Joe brought the car back, he intended to be waiting, whether his mission was accomplished or not.

A bell rang as he pushed open the door, and a handful of wind chimes rustled in the breeze. His entry attracted the attention of both the women by the counter, and the child regarded him solemnly, its thumb pushed into its mouth.

It only took a moment to realise that neither of the women was Isobel Herriot. He had hardly expected her to be the young mother anyway, but the girl behind the counter looked like a teenager. His spirits plummeted, the determination that had driven him through the door bringing a resigned droop to his mouth. He might have known it wouldn't be that easy. Nothing ever was.

'Hello.' The girl behind the counter was regarding him with a rather avid interest, and although he wasn't a conceited man he suspected that there was a certain covetousness in her gaze. 'Are you looking for Issy?' she asked, desecrating what Patrick had previously thought of as a

very attractive name. 'She's in the back. I'll get her. She
was just about to go for lunch.

'I—well—'

She was gone before he could stop her, and the young
woman hanging onto the toddler gave him a reassuring look.
'Nice day, isn't it?' she asked. 'If only we could get rid of
that wind. Still, it dries the clothes, and saves the electricity. That's what my husband always says.'

Patrick smiled, and only someone who knew him rather
better than she did would have known that his smile wasn't
genuine. 'At least it's fine,' he managed smoothly, wondering why the English always talked about the weather.
He looked down and saw that the little girl had snatched
what looked like a handful of dried leaves out of an open
barrel and was about to stuff them into her mouth. He
nodded. 'I think your daughter's trying to tell you something. It's lunchtime for her too, I guess.'

'What? Ooh, Tracy!' The young woman bent down and
tipped the crushed debris out of her hand. 'That's pot
pourri,' she added, pronouncing it so that it rhymed with
'hot fury'. 'Aunty Chris will get into trouble if you're
naughty like that again.'

Patrick was turning away to prevent himself from grinning
at the youngster, when Isobel came out of the room at the
back of the shop. The other girl was following her, smiling
and quirking her eyebrows at the woman with the toddler.
He supposed Isobel must have told her assistant that he had
come back to collect the necklace, but he couldn't believe
they got so few customers that his purchase was unique.

She was wearing a floral print today, a dress this time,
but with a similarly long hem. As she came around the end
of the counter and handed him a package, he saw that the
heavy boots were still in evidence, together with a denim
haversack over one shoulder, which added to her outdoor
appearance.

'There you are,' she said, apparently undisturbed by the
stares from the other women. 'I've put a ribbon on it. I
thought she might like it to look special.'

'She?'

For a minute, Patrick was confused. The delicate aroma of her perfume had surrounded him again, and he was intensely conscious of the nearness of her body. The dress had short sleeves and a V neckline, and in the opening he could see the dusky hollow between her breasts. He could smell the faint heat of her skin, too, as she turned aside from him, her mission apparently completed.

'Your niece.'

Her response drifted over her shoulder, and he struggled to pull himself together as what she had said suddenly made sense. 'Oh, yes, my niece,' he agreed mechanically, weighing the gift-wrapped package between his fingers. 'Um—thank you,' he added lamely. 'I'm sure she'll be delighted.'

Liar.

He knew, just as he'd known when he'd bought the necklace two days ago, that Susie would never see it. He supposed he could pretend he'd bought it elsewhere, but it was too big a risk to take. Besides, it wasn't as if it had been expensive. He could have been stuck with a bill for a piece of jewellery if Isobel had worked for a goldsmith. As it was, he had his parcel and no further need to stay.

Or so *she* thought.

But what the hell could he do with the other two women watching his reactions so closely? What were they expecting? he wondered. What had she told them about him? He found that he resented the thought that she had apparently been discussing him with her young assistant. Had they been speculating about his identity? Or was it something more personal than that?

There was nothing for it but to leave. Even if he'd been inclined to ask to speak to her privately—in the back room, perhaps—he found the idea repulsive. He had no way of knowing how soundproof the walls of the room might be, and the thought of their discussion being overheard in the shop was too abhorrent to consider.

'Was there something else?'

Isobel was waiting for him to go, and with a terse shake of his head Patrick strode towards the door. So much for his hopes of dealing with the matter swiftly, he thought.

Now he was going to have to think of an excuse to come back again.

He was stepping out into the sunlight when he realised she was behind him, and he suddenly remembered that the girl—Chris?—had said Isobel was just about to go for lunch. Which explained the ugly haversack, he supposed. Why couldn't she use a handbag like anyone else?

He moved aside to hold the door for her, and although he sensed she didn't welcome his assistance she was too polite to ignore the courtesy. 'Thanks,' she said, with a tight smile, and started off along the pavement. And, before common sense could prevent the gesture, Patrick caught hold of her arm.

'Excuse me . . .'

'Yes?'

Her response warned him she was not in the mood for any prevarication, and Patrick said the first thing that came into his head. 'Um—I don't suppose you'd consider having lunch with me? I've—got a business proposition I'd like to put to you.'

CHAPTER FOUR

ISOBEL sucked in her breath. 'A business proposition?' she echoed sceptically. 'What kind of a business proposition?'

The man glanced up and down the high street. 'Well, I'd prefer not to discuss it here,' he remarked, his eyes returning to her face. 'Your—assistant said it was your lunch break. It would seem to kill two birds with one stone if we ate together.'

Would it?

Isobel moistened her lips with a nervous tongue. 'But— I don't even know your name,' she protested uneasily. 'And, honestly, Mr—er—well, I don't really think you're interested in Caprice.'

Which seemed to imply he was interested in her, she realised unhappily as soon as the words were spoken. And she was fairly sure that that wasn't the case at all. Whatever he had on his mind, it wasn't the seduction of her rather too generous body. She'd seen him looking at her breasts, and she doubted he was attracted by their wholesome exuberance. Besides, like Richard, he was wearing a ring on the third finger of his left hand. His wife was probably one of those elegant clothes-horses, with angular bones and a narrow chest.

'You're wrong,' he said firmly. 'And my name's...Riker—Patrick Riker.' He held out his hand, and she was obliged to take it. 'There, now,' he added, with a wry smile, 'we're properly introduced.'

Isobel managed a brief smile in return, but as soon as she could she pulled her hand away. It wasn't that she didn't like touching his flesh; on the contrary, his skin felt disturbingly intimate gripping her damp palm. But it was this, more than anything, that made her wary. She'd never felt so aware of another individual before.

'So...lunch?' he reminded her, holding her gaze with eyes that were green in some lights and hazel in others. The wind lifted a lock of dark hair and deposited it on his forehead. Patrick Riker—if that really was his name— pushed it back with long, olive-skinned fingers, drawing her attention to the length of the hair that brushed the virgin whiteness of his collar.

Only she suspected there was nothing remotely virgin about him. There was too much knowledge—too much experience—in that lean, intelligent face. He wasn't strictly handsome; his features—high cheekbones, a narrow blade of a nose, a thin, almost cruel mouth—were too strong for that. But there was no doubt that he was attractive; she was sure that women must fall over themselves trying to capture his attention.

'Well, I don't usually eat lunch,' she said at last, having no intention of telling him that she usually went home during her lunch break. All the same, it was quite pleasant to have to look up at a man. At five feet eight herself, it wasn't usually the case.

'Make an exception,' he persisted, casting another swift glance along the length of the high street. 'Oh—excuse me a moment. I have to speak to someone. Just wait here. This won't take very long.'

Isobel sighed. This was becoming ridiculous. Why couldn't he just accept that she didn't want to have lunch with him? Just because he was used to getting his own way it was no reason for her to bolster his ego.

Her awareness of eyes boring into her back made her turn her head. Christine and her sister were peering around the tastefully designed pyramid of scented candles she'd just arranged that morning. Evidently they had seen him talking to her, and were watching eagerly to see what happened next. Well, they were going to be disappointed, she decided. She was not going to provide a peep-show for anyone.

Patrick Riker had crossed the pavement, and was presently leaning in the window of a large green limousine that was parked at the kerb. The driver of the limousine was a black man, she noticed unwilling. Was that the car Chris had spoken about—the swish vehicle she'd thought was a Rolls-Royce?

She wasn't interested.

Jamming her teeth together, Isobel strode quickly to the first intersection. It had occurred to her that, as Patrick Riker didn't know his way around Horsham, if she could disappear into a side-street she could very likely give him the slip. She might even be able to make her way home, if she used a roundabout route. It was annoying that she was having to do this, but she didn't believe he wanted to speak to her about her business at all.

So what did he want to speak to her about? She tapped her foot impatiently as a delivery wagon took an inordinate amount of time to clear the junction. She wasn't absurdly modest, but she wasn't credulous either. He hadn't bought the necklace because he fancied her. He was far too sophisticated for that.

'Isobel—*Miss Herriot*!'

He had seen her. Even as she contemplated pretending she hadn't heard his call, the powerful limousine swept by her, with only the driver on board. Already Patrick Riker's powerful strides were eating up the ground between them. She could wait for him, or she could run. Somehow the latter seemed vaguely childish.

'Is something wrong?' he asked when he reached her, and she looked at him with irritation in her eyes.

'I thought I'd explained—I don't have time to eat lunch,' she said, preparing to cross the street. 'Thank you for your invitation, but I've got more important things to do.'

'More important than expanding your business?' he asked, taking her breath away with the scope of his suggestion. 'I'm in a position to offer you another outlet. In—Stratford, let's say, if that appeals to you.'

Isobel swallowed. 'Why?'

He looked a little taken aback at that, but he recovered quickly, and moved his shoulders in a dismissive gesture. 'Why not?' he countered. 'It seems a worthwhile proposition.' He paused. 'We could discuss it at more length if you'd agree to join me for lunch.'

Isobel tried to think. 'I—I can't.'

'Why can't you?'

'Because—' she consulted the rather mannish watch on her wrist '—I've got to be back at the shop in half an hour. Chris—my assistant—only works part-time. I promised I wouldn't be long.'

Which was at least partially true. Chris did only work part-time, and she had said she wouldn't be long. But she had no doubt that Chris would understand if she was late. Particularly if she thought her employer was having lunch with *him*.

His hesitation was only momentary. 'Dinner, then,' he said, his lips thinning as if the idea was as alien to him as it was to her. 'Have dinner with me this evening. I'd very much like to talk to you.'

Isobel hesitated now. Common sense advised her to refuse his invitation, but, deep inside, some rebellious instinct was urging her to accept. What did she have to lose, after all? It wasn't as if she was in any danger of falling for him. She should take the opportunity to be wined and dined by an attractive man at its face value. At the least, she'd probably enjoy the meal, and it was always possible that he did mean what he said.

'All right,' she said, her tongue once again acting several seconds ahead of her brain. 'Um—where shall we go? I'll meet you.' She cast her mind around. 'There's pub at Swalford called The Coach House. It's only about a mile away. How about that?'

'Sounds good.' His expression softened. 'But why don't I pick you up? That way we can both have a drink.'

'It's all right. I don't drink much anyway,' declared Isobel hurriedly. She had no desire for him to find out where she lived. 'I'll meet you there at—at half past seven. Or is that too early for you? I can't make it any sooner because the shop doesn't close until six o'clock.'

'No problem.' The wind ruffled his hair again, and he swept it back with an impatient hand. 'Until half past seven, then. I'll be looking forward to it.'

Isobel smiled, but she didn't make a similar claim. Now that the arrangements were made, she was suffering the usual feelings of doubt about her decision. Why had she

agreed to meet him when she believed his motives were
suspect? Somehow, the justification that she had nothing
to lose no longer convinced her.

Isobel got home that evening later than she had anticipated. Several Japanese tourists, who had been visiting the
monastery, had discovered the shop on the way back to the
coach, and because of language difficulties their purchases
had taken rather longer then she would have liked. Of
course, they were charming people, and unfailingly polite,
but by the time Isobel had ushered the last pair out of the
door it was already quarter past six.

One way and another, it had been a frustrating day, she
thought tensely, and it wasn't over yet. She still had to decide
what she was going to wear tonight, and the prospect of
the evening ahead filled her with unease.

Still, she was committed to going, and according to Chris,
who had insisted on hearing all the details, she should make
the most of it. Whatever his motives, her young assistant
had told her, Patrick Riker was the most exciting man *she*
had ever met, and if Isobel wanted a substitute she'd happily
go in her place.

Of course, that was out of the question, and Chris knew
it. But that hadn't stopped her offering Isobel advice on
everything from the clothes she should choose to the make-
up she should wear.

'Put on some of that Champagne perfume,' she'd suggested, mentioning the expensive Yves Saint Laurent
fragrance her parents had bought her for her birthday. 'And
for goodness' sake don't put your hair in that braid. Leave
it loose, for once. It suits you.'

Now, half an hour later, Isobel surveyed the pile of dis-
carded garments lying on the bed with raw impatience. It
was no use; she had nothing suitable for spending an evening
with a man like him. She had thought her navy suit would
do, but that looked incredibly formal, and her dresses were
all cotton, and most of them had seen better days.

All she was left with were the full skirts and loose shirts
she usually wore for working in. Most of the time, when

she wasn't wearing her long skirts or cotton dresses, she wore jeans and sweaters. But, like everything else she'd pulled out of her wardrobe, the jeans were worn and shabby. Her mother was right; she should spend more time on herself. But that wasn't going to help her now.

With an irritated gesture, she snatched up the least boring item on the bed and put it on. As a matter of fact, it was also her least favourite garment, which was probably why it didn't look as tired as the rest. It was a sleeveless pinafore, made of fine black cotton jersey, which she'd previously only worn with a T-shirt underneath. But tonight she allowed the spaghetti straps to rest on her smooth bare shoulders, the button-through bodice moulding the curves that she tried so hard to ignore.

She sighed. It was a warm evening, and despite her misgivings the dress was not unsuitable. But it was far more revealing than anything she had owned before, and she was about to tear it off again when someone knocked at her door.

'Oh, damn!' she groaned, hoping against hope that it wasn't Richard. After the way she'd sent him away on Tuesday evening, it would be typical of him to turn up unannounced. She didn't want to have to tell him she was going out with another man, particularly a man she hardly knew, and for whom she was making such a fuss.

She stood by her bed, hoping whoever it was would get the message and go away again, but, as before, the knocker was rapped once more. Of course, it could be her mother, she thought. It was almost a week since she'd seen either of her parents, and they were unlikely to hold her up, particularly if they thought she had a heavy date. Not that it was heavy, she reminded herself, but her mother wasn't to know that.

Deciding she would have to see who it was, she ran hastily down the stairs. Because of the angle of the eaves, it was impossible to spy on the porch from the bedroom, and she could hardly peer through the living-room window and risk coming face to face with a stranger. She could have looked out of the window upstairs to see if there was a strange car

parked in the lane. But as she had no garage herself she
had to park at her gate, and visitors to the church sometimes used what free space was left.

Of course, she acknowledged as soon as she opened the
door, she would have recognised Patrick Riker's car if she'd
seen it. Its width alone was making it very difficult for any
other car to pass along the narrow lane, and its dark green
elegance was unmistakable. The man, too, was fairly unforgettable, propped rather indolently against her porch.
He was still wearing the dark blue suit he had worn that
afternoon, and in light of the fact that she'd arranged to
meet him later on her lips tightened impatiently at his
presumption.

'Hi,' he said, not at all put out by her obvious annoyance. 'I was early, so I thought I might as well come
and fetch you after all.' His eyes narrowed. 'You look nice.
And ready, too, if I'm not mistaken.'

Isobel knew a childish impulse to stamp her foot. He had
no right to come here, no right to know where she lived—
though she could guess who had given him her address. No
wonder Chris had looked so smug when she'd announced
she was having dinner with him. She probably already knew.

'Well, I'm not quite,' she stated now. 'Ready, I mean.'
She paused. 'Why don't you go on ahead? I can give you
directions from here.'

'Without you?' he protested. 'I'd rather wait.' He looked
beyond her, into the sun-dappled hall behind her. 'I don't
mind.'

Isobel pressed her lips together. 'As you like,' she declared tersely, and shut the door in his face.

It was rude, perhaps, but she didn't know him, she defended herself as she went back upstairs. Women were
always being advised not to invite virtual strangers into their
home. Besides, his—what? Chauffeur? Bodyguard?—was
bound to get impatient. They could keep one another
company. It wasn't her fault he had changed the
arrangements.

But the black dress would have to do, she conceded, with
a sigh. She had no intention of changing again and giving

him the impression she was fussy about what she wore. Some eyeshadow, a little mascara and a caramel-coloured lipstick achieved the effect she was seeking, and she finally picked up her hairbrush to try and subdue the sun-streaked tangle of her hair.

Chris had said not to put it in the braid, but she wasn't at all sure she wanted to give her young assistant credit for anything. In the event, she secured it at her nape with a velvet scrunch band, aware that curling tendrils would soon escape the constriction and cluster about her temples and her neck.

It was daunting to emerge from the cottage and lock her door with Patrick Riker's eyes upon her. And his companion's eyes, she appended tersely. She wasn't used to being watched, and she didn't like it. She was glad she had wrapped a black and white Paisley scarf about her shoulders. Although it was a warm evening, it didn't make her feel so exposed.

However, when she approached the car, she discovered that Patrick was alone. He emerged from behind the wheel to open the front passenger door for her, and she realised that for all her caution they were still to spend some time alone.

'Where's your—er—?'

She faltered over the designation, and Patrick helped her out. 'Joe?' he asked. 'His name's Joe Muzambe. And I've given him the evening off.' He closed her door and walked around to fold his length in beside her. He looked her way. 'Is it a problem?'

Put like that, it would have sounded rather churlish to object. Besides, it was less than a mile to Swalford. She could always get a taxi home if she thought he'd had too much to drink.

She shook her head, feeling the recalcitrant strands of hair squeezing out of the band already. 'I—assumed he'd be driving,' she said, hoping that didn't sound as if she'd expected it. It wasn't as if she was used to riding around in expensive cars, with or without a chauffeur at the wheel.

'Don't you trust me?' he asked, and she realised he had not been deceived by her reticence. 'I know I can't prove it, but you're perfectly safe with me.'

Of course she was.

'I didn't—that is, I hope you don't think—'

'What?' His eyes were narrowed now. 'What are you trying to say? That you don't like me?' He started the engine, his mouth curling into an ironic smile. 'That's all right. It's not a prerequisite for doing business with someone.'

Isobel took a deep breath. 'That's not what I meant.'

'No?'

His answer was hardly satisfactory, but the lane was clear of traffic, and he pulled away before she could say any more. Beyond the cottage the lane narrowed, before turning right into another lane that eventually intersected with the high street. It was not a well-known route, but Horsham was not a large village, and most roads ultimately led back to where you'd started. Nevertheless she had the feeling that he'd already checked it out before he even knocked at her door.

'No,' she said now, and added with a faint edge to her voice as he turned left along the high street, 'You seem to know your way around.'

The look he gave her was slightly wary, and she wondered what she'd said to arouse his distrust. It was a free country, for heaven's sake, and for all she knew he might know the area better than she did. But she had the feeling he was a stranger. She was sure she'd have heard about him if he'd moved into the district.

'I just follow the signposts,' he remarked after a moment, and she had to admit there had been an arrow pointing towards Swalford at the junction.

There was silence for a few moments after that, Isobel struggling desperately to think of something suitable to say. It wasn't that she wanted him to think her particularly clever, but she didn't want him to think she was stupid either. The trouble was, the men she usually went out with were locals, and she doubted Patrick Riker would be interested in the fact that they were having a drought.

He drove fairly slowly through the village, but once out of the restricted area he allowed the car to find its own speed. The roads around Horsham were inclined to be a little twisty, so there was no question of racing, but he covered the three-quarters of a mile to Swalford in an amazingly short time.

'I guess this is it,' he remarked finally, turning into the car park of the The Coach House and parking beside an old Mercedes that had seen better days. For all it was quite early in the evening, there were quite a few cars already occupying the inn's forecourt—an indication of the popularity of its bar food.

'I hope you won't find it a disappointment,' murmured Isobel, barely audibly, as she acknowledged the incongruity of the limousine in these surroundings. But he'd heard her, and his lips twitched at the back-handed compliment.

'I doubt if anything could disappoint me this evening,' he assured her with equal ambiguity. Then, more gently, he asked, 'Shall we go in?'

CHAPTER FIVE

A HAZE of tobacco smoke hung over the bar, but the dining area adjoined a flagged patio, and the doors had been flung wide to admit the evening air. There were tables on the patio, too, and Patrick allowed her to choose where she wanted to sit. Isobel opted for a table that was near the open doors but not actually on the patio, and Patrick went to get them a drink while she perused the menu.

She had chosen white wine to drink, and he came back with a glass for her and a bottle of imported beer for himself. Pulling out the wooden chair opposite her, he sank into it, accepting the menu she passed him and glancing carelessly at its contents.

'I suppose this isn't what you're used to,' she said a little awkwardly, despising herself for caring what he thought. She hadn't instigated this meeting; he had. If he didn't like her choice of venue, hard luck.

'You don't know what I'm used to,' he countered, lifting his eyes from the menu. 'Am I allowed to ask what you're eating? Or is that a state secret?'

Isobel expelled her breath. 'Lasagne,' she said. 'With a green salad to start.' She licked her lips. 'They make it on the premises. The owner's wife comes from Siena.'

'Ah.' His eyes dropped back to the menu. 'You don't fancy a fillet steak, or anything carnivorous like that?'

'Well, I'm not a vegetarian,' she retorted, 'if that's what you're implying. It's not a vegetable lasagne. It does contain meat.'

'All right.' His tone was amused now. 'I'll have that too. And a bottle of claret, just to prove I'm not a cheapskate. I can imagine what my chauffeur would say if he knew I'd turned down the steak.'

42

Isobel looked up at him through her lashes, not quite sure what to make of that, and he grinned. She'd thought he was attractive before, but when his face creased into that infectious smile her heart seemed to skip a beat. Dear God, she thought uneasily, picking up her glass of wine and taking a rather unwary sip, Chris was right—he was devastating.

And dangerous.

He left to order the meal, which would be brought to their table when it was ready, and Isobel wondered when he'd get around to the reason why they had come. It was pleasant to delude herself with the thought that he found her company enjoyable, but, whatever else, he was married, and she had to remember that.

'This is very nice,' he said a few moments later, resuming his seat, and Isobel made the usual response.

'It's busier than this when the children break up for the summer holidays,' she said, indicating the few empty tables. 'There's a caravan site not far from here, and the pub attracts a lot of evening visitors.'

Patrick nodded. 'At the risk of sounding trite, do you come here often?'

'Not often,' she conceded. 'Maybe half a dozen times a year.' She wondered if she should go on, and then continued carefully, 'I don't go out a lot. I'm not a night person.'

Patrick's eyes were too intent. 'There's no regular boyfriend, then?'

She caught her breath. 'I don't think that's any of your business.'

'And if I wanted to make it my business?'

'You can't.' She hesitated a moment. 'You're married.' She held up her head. 'Don't you think we ought to talk about why you've brought me here? Or was that just a ploy?'

'How do you know I'm married?' he probed, choosing the least appropriate thing she'd said, and Isobel looked down at her glass.

'Does it matter?' she asked uncomfortably, wishing she'd just made a simple refusal. 'Oh—thank you,' she said as the waitress appeared with their salads. 'No dressing for me. This is fine.'

Patrick refused the dressing too, she noticed, and then moved immediately back into the attack. 'It matters,' he said softly, and she was aware of his eyes upon her. 'Apart from anything else, I'm curious. Humour me.'

Isobel sighed. 'You're wearing a wedding ring,' she said at last, tersely. 'Now, can we get on with the food?'

'It's not a wedding ring,' he insisted. 'It was—once. But not any longer. I've been divorced for almost six years.'

'Really?'

'Yes, really.' He touched her hand as it rested on the table. 'Don't you believe me?'

'If—if you say so, then of course I believe you. But, as I said before, I don't think it matters either way.'

He caught his lower lip between his teeth. 'Does that mean you wouldn't go out with a married man?'

'I—' Isobel was essentially honest, and she had to admit that if he asked her she'd be tempted. 'I—suppose not,' she finished lamely, and he looked suddenly grim.

They ate the rest of their salad in silence, and she had the feeling that once again she'd said something he didn't like. Did that mean that he was lying? Was he really married, after all? Or had her doubts communicated themselves to him, and he was shocked?

But no. She didn't believe that. She sensed that she'd have to say something pretty outrageous to shock this man. So what was he thinking? What was causing that sudden darkness to etch his features? And why did she care anyway? She'd probably never see him again.

'Did—er—did your niece like the necklace?' she asked, eager to change the subject, and for a moment she thought he wasn't going to answer her.

But then, after a pregnant pause, he said, 'I haven't given it to her yet. She—er—she doesn't live in London.'

'Is that where you live?' she asked, deciding she had the right to ask some questions of her own, and after a moment he gave a resigned nod.

'That's right,' he said, without expression. 'But it's good to get out of the city now and again.'

'To Warwickshire?' she prompted, and his features grew less tense.

'Among other places,' he agreed easily. 'Do you travel much, Miss Herriot? Or do you prefer the rural life?'

Isobel found she resented his assumption that Horsham must encompass her whole world, and, as if glimpsing the conflicting emotions she was trying hard to suppress, he added gently, 'It wasn't a criticism. If you're happy here, I envy you. I've been striving all my life to find true peace of mind.'

Isobel gave him a retiring look. 'I think you're patronising me.'

'I assure you I'm not.'

'You expect me to believe that?'

'Why not? It's the truth.' He paused. 'As you get to know me better you'll find I almost always speak the truth.'

'*Almost* always?'

'I'm in business,' he said mildly. 'There have to be exceptions. It wouldn't do for me to reveal all my secrets.'

Isobel couldn't resist a small smile. 'What kind of business are you in?'

'What kind of—?' He broke off abruptly, before continuing rather less incredulously, 'Um—this and that. I—buy and sell things, mostly. Here and overseas.'

'Here?' She frowned. 'As in Horsham?'

'I meant here in England,' he replied. 'But you didn't answer my question: do you prefer the country life?'

'I suppose I must.' Isobel hesitated, and then went on reluctantly, 'I lived in London for a time. After I'd got my degree. But it didn't work out, and I came back here.'

She guessed he was curious about what she had done while she'd been living in London, but the return of the waitress with the wine forestalled any questions. 'The lasagne is just coming,' she said, removing their salad plates, and Patrick poured two glasses of the rich dark liquid and took a sip.

'Mmm, that's good,' he said, pushing Isobel's glass towards her, and she wondered if she was only imagining the condescension in his tone.

'For a village pub, you mean?' she suggested tartly, and he gave her a resigned look.

'No. By any standards,' he retorted, watching as she tasted hers. 'Don't be so defensive. I'm not an expert.'

'Is that supposed to be a vindication?' she exclaimed, though she couldn't hide her enjoyment of the wine he'd chosen. 'Are you one of those people who justify their—well, who say, "I know what I like"?'

'Justify their ignorance?' he countered at once, disconcerting her now. 'Let's stop insulting one another, shall we? Tell me where you worked in London.'

Isobel sighed. She had hoped not to have to discuss her job in London, or the reason why she had left. 'As a matter of fact, I worked for Aychbourn's,' she admitted at last. 'But I didn't like it, so I left.'

'Aychbourn's? The auctioneers?' He was impressed.

'Mmm.' Isobel wished they could get off the subject. 'I'm not such a country bumpkin after all.'

'I never thought you were!' he exclaimed. 'Aychbourn's, eh?' He frowned. 'Did you ever meet a man called Charlie Ankrum?'

Isobel moistened her dry lips. '*Mr* Ankrum was my boss,' she declared stiffly. She might have known Patrick Riker would know him. They were probably two of a kind:

'Really?' he said. Then, perceptively, he asked, 'You didn't like him?'

'It wasn't my place to like or dislike him,' she replied primly. 'Oh—here's the lasagne,' she added with some relief. 'Doesn't it look good?'

It was good, as always, but Isobel found it impossible to enjoy hers. It had occurred to her that if Patrick Riker was serious about the offer he had made at lunchtime—and which so far he hadn't mentioned—he would require a reference, and she could just imagine what Charles Ankrum would have to say about her. 'Oh, yes, she's an adequate worker,' she could imagine him confiding in his lazy, public-school drawl, 'but she's hopelessly provincial. We did our best with her, but she couldn't cut it, old man, and that's the truth.'

'Was he the reason you left?' Patrick asked at last, when she'd begun to think he'd forgotten all about Aychbourn's and Charles Ankrum, and Isobel sighed.

'My grandmother died and left me some money,' she said, which wasn't quite what he'd asked. 'I was tired of living in the city, so I decided to come home.'

Patrick forked the last morsel of his lasagne into his mouth, and breathed a sigh of satisfaction. 'That was excellent,' he declared, so that for a moment she thought he had accepted her answer. But then he said, 'I wondered if Charlie had been up to his old tricks again. He has quite a reputation for sleaze.'

Isobel caught her breath. 'I thought he was a friend of yours.'

'Why? Because I know him?' Patrick grimaced. 'I know a lot of people, Isobel. I don't have to like them all.'

She shivered. It wasn't what he had said so much as the casual way he had used her name. She didn't mind him using it; she found she liked the sound of it on his tongue. The trace of what she thought might be an Irish accent gave his voice an attractive brogue, though she guessed he had been brought up in England for all that.

'Was it all right?'

The waitress was back to clear the dirty dishes, and she looked askance at Isobel's plate. 'Oh—yes,' said Isobel guiltily, her cheeks suffusing with colour. 'I'm afraid I wasn't very hungry. It must be the heat.'

'Or me,' remarked Patrick quietly, when the woman had departed. 'I'm sure you don't normally eat like a fly.'

Isobel raised her eyebrows. 'Is that a polite way of saying I'm fat?'

'No.' For a moment he thought she was serious, and then he realised she was teasing him and laughed. 'You look in pretty good shape to me. And—' he held up a warning hand '—before you say I'm patronising you again, I'm not.'

Isobel's colour refused to subside, and she took refuge in her glass. It would be so easy to like him, so easy to delude herself that he had some personal interest in her. And even if he was briefly attracted by her novelty value it would be unwise for her to get involved with someone like him—someone who could only bring her grief.

'Anyway,' he said, after a few moments, 'I suppose we should get down to business. About this shop in Stratford; does the idea appeal to you?'

Isobel endeavoured to control herself. 'I—well, of course it appeals to me,' she admitted, though until that moment she hadn't really thought much about it. It was true that she was finding it increasingly difficult now to find room for all the stock she was being offered, and another shop would ease the load. She might even begin to specialise, selling only soft goods in one shop and hard goods in the other. There would certainly be more opportunities in a busy tourist spot like Shakespeare's birthplace, although the initial outlay would be correspondingly higher. Which was why she'd never considered it before.

'So how much floor and storage space would you need?' Patrick asked seriously. 'How much do you have at the current shop? I accept the fact that the Stratford shop would have to be bigger. There's not much point in moving into smaller premises.'

Isobel's narrow brows drew together. 'Did you say *moving*?'

Patrick blinked. 'Moving into larger premises, yes.'

'You mean you expect me to close the shop in Horsham?' Isobel stared at him. 'I thought you meant I should open another branch.'

Patrick's mouth tightened. 'Did I say that?'

'You said, did I want to expand my business? What else was I supposed to think?'

He sighed. 'Then I'm afraid you misunderstood me. I assumed larger premises in a larger town would be enough.'

'For a *provincial* shopkeeper?' said Isobel sarcastically, and had the unwilling satisfaction of seeing deep colour flood into his dark cheeks.

'For anyone,' he retorted shortly, clearly not used to being wrong-footed. 'I'm sorry if you think I deliberately misled you. I can assure you that wasn't my intention.'

'So what was your intention, Mr Riker?' Isobel demanded in a low voice, aware that her previous remark had been delivered several octaves higher. 'What possible advantage would my moving to Stratford be to you?'

His nostrils flared. 'The advantage would be all yours.'

'Really?' She didn't believe a word of it, but the alternative—that he had used this proposition as bait to get her to come out with him—didn't seem credible either.

'Yes, really,' he declared harshly. 'You have an extremely low opinion of my sex, Miss Herriot. I wonder what Charlie Ankrum really did to you?'

Isobel had no intention of discussing Charles Ankrum's disgusting suggestions with him. 'I think I'd like to go home now,' she said instead, shifting her scarf, which had fallen onto her seat behind her, back onto her shoulders. 'I can get a cab, if you'd rather stay and finish your wine.'

'And be accused of having ulterior motives?' he demanded drily as she got to her feet. 'No, I'm ready to go,' he added, flexing his back beside her. 'Just give me a couple of minutes to pay the bill.'

It was still light when he joined her outside. The air was soft and velvety, and even the smell of food, drifting from the tables set outdoors, was not unpleasant. But the scent of woodsmoke was nicer, and the disturbed clatter of a pheasant as it fluttered out of harm's way was more attractive than the sound of knives and forks. All the sights and sounds of a summer evening, thought Isobel ruefully. What a pity it had to end on such a sour note.

Because she had enjoyed herself. Until Patrick had started talking about the shop, she'd been having a good time. Which was ironic really when the shop was the whole point of her being there. And dangerous, too. Despite all the warnings she'd given herself, he'd still managed to get under her guard.

She slipped into the car without his assistance, and he took off his jacket and tossed it onto the back seat before getting in beside her. She was intensely aware of the darkness of his skin beneath the fine fabric of his shirt, and of the triangle of dark hair that was etched across his chest.

The scent of his heated skin came to her as he unbuttoned the collar of his shirt and pulled the loop of his tie a couple of inches away. It was a disturbing smell, clean and masculine, with just a trace of musk to prove his pores were working overtime.

She wanted to say something, anything, to break the sudden tension that had developed between them. She knew he must be angry, but he was doing a good job of hiding his feelings. Yet it wasn't her fault that he'd misjudged the situation. She just wished she knew what his real motives had been.

Once again, the insidious thought that he might be interested in her invaded her consciousness. Ludicrous as it seemed, she didn't know what else to think. If it was something to do with Shannon Holdings wanting vacant possession of all the shops in the row, surely someone else would have heard of it. And why pick on her, when there were older, less assertive tenants than herself to intimidate?

In any case, Richard would have warned her if there was going to be a problem. He was the company's representative, after all, and she suspected he'd do anything to ingratiate himself with her. Patrick Riker had singled her out for attention, so what was she to think?

The realisation that the car was drawing to a halt was her first indication that she was home. She'd been so absorbed with the reason why Patrick Riker should have taken her out, she'd been totally unaware that he'd brought her back. But here she was, just a few yards from her gate, and the evening was almost over.

She turned to offer her thanks and surprised a curious look on his face. It was an expression that seemed to mingle impatience and frustration in equal measures, and she wondered what he was thinking, and why he felt the need to disguise his true feelings.

Still, it seemed to explode the myth of her attraction for him, and she took a deep breath and made a polite attempt to show her gratitude, for the meal if nothing else. 'I did enjoy it,' she said, feeling something of a hypocrite. 'Thank you for bringing me home.'

'My pleasure.'

He inclined his head, but Isobel was aware that that wasn't precisely the truth. 'Um—would you like some coffee?' she found herself asking, and then knew a moment's horror at her own insanity. For God's sake, hadn't she just been berating herself for falling under his spell? She didn't want him in her house—she *didn't*! She didn't want his image anywhere but at the shop.

'No, thanks.' She didn't know whether to be affronted or relieved by his instant rejection. 'I've got an early start in the morning, so I guess I'd better get back to the hotel.' He paused, and then leaned towards her and bestowed a light kiss on the corner of her mouth. 'Can I give you a ring next time I'm in the area?'

CHAPTER SIX

IT WAS after eleven when the plane landed. They'd been late leaving New York, and although the pilot had made up some of the time lag on the journey they were still approximately forty minutes late into Heathrow.

Joe was waiting for him. As Patrick came into the arrivals hall, he saw the burly chauffeur standing patiently beside the barrier. He lifted his hand in greeting when he saw his employer, and came around the end of the railings to take the luggage trolley.

'Good trip?' he asked, steering his way towards the door, and Patrick nodded.

'Not bad,' he said flatly. 'Where's the car?'

The Bentley was parked at the kerb, running the gauntlet of double yellow lines and traffic wardens alike. Joe loaded Patrick's case into the boot and then came to take his seat behind the wheel. Patrick had already taken the seat beside him, weariness precluding any inclination he might have felt to work.

Despite the lateness of the hour, the roads around the airport were still fairly busy, but Joe soon had them safely onto the M4. On the outskirts of the city, he used his local knowledge to avoid the bottleneck of the Hammersmith flyover, and less than twenty minutes after leaving the motorway he was setting Patrick down outside his Central London home.

'Thanks.'

Patrick patted the man's shoulder as he got out of the car, and Joe gave his usual laid-back grin. 'What time in the morning?' he asked. 'I assume you will be going into the office, even though Mrs Gregory's been agitating to see you ever since you went away.'

Patrick's mouth thinned. 'Mrs Gregory will have to wait,' he declared, picking up his flight bag and the leather carrier that held his suits. He'd avoided any confrontation with Jillian before he'd gone away, and he was in no hurry to precipitate one now. 'See you in the morning. Usual time.'

Despite an annoying conviction that he wouldn't sleep well, Patrick was still sound asleep when his phone rang at seven-thirty the next morning. Dragging himself up out of a jet-lagged slumber, and cursing whatever crisis had entailed this summons, he was not best pleased when he discovered it was his sister on the line. 'Do you know what time it is?' he snarled, glaring at the phone as if she could see him. 'For God's sake, Jill, let me get back into the country, will you?'

'You got back into the country last night,' she retorted, resentful that he should speak to her that way. 'I thought you might have rung me. You must have got my messages. That big hunk Muzambe said he was going to meet you himself.'

Patrick squashed the impulse to say that Joe should keep his bloody mouth shut, and took a deep breath to calm down. But, dammit, his heart was racing, and he had the beginnings of a headache, due no doubt to being so rudely aroused from sleep.

'The plane was late,' he said, aware that he was defending himself when no defence was necessary. 'I didn't think you'd want me to wake you at midnight.'

Jillian sighed. 'Oh—well, I suppose you have a point. But you are coming out to see us, aren't you? Mum says you haven't been to Kerrymore for weeks.'

Patrick closed his eyes. 'I don't know about coming to Oxford, Jill. I have been away for over a week, and the work's piling up in the office. I'd like to see you—and Mum—you know that. I just don't think I—'

'He's still seeing her, you know!'

Jillian's choked intervention put paid to any hopes he might have had of stealing another half-hour's sleep. 'Who, Richard?' he asked, but he knew. There was no one else Jillian cared about with quite so much fervour, and the

space he'd thought he'd put between himself and Isobel
Herriot was instantly breached.

'Of course Richard!' she exclaimed, her hushed tone revealing that her husband was still in the house. 'He was
there again on Thursday. They spent the night at some pub
called The Coach House.'

It was like a blow to his gut, and Patrick almost winced
at the sudden nausea he felt. 'They spent the *night* at The
Coach House?' he said faintly. Then, recovering rapidly,
he asked, 'How do you know? Have you put a private de-
tective on his back?'

'No.' Jillian sounded almost scandalised. 'But I found
the receipt for the room in his pocket. The Coach House,
Swalford. I don't think I'll ever forget that name. Oh, Pat,
you've got to do something. I'm going out of my mind.'

He knew the feeling. 'Jill, we've gone over this before.
Short of confronting him myself, there's not much I can
do.'

'You still won't evict her, then? Not even for me?' Jillian
caught her breath on a sob. 'There's no one I can turn to
but you.'

Patrick groaned. 'Jill—'

'You said you'd speak to her before you went away,' she
reminded him tearfully. 'And I know the reason you've been
avoiding my calls is because you feel guilty—'

'*Guilty?*'

'For not speaking to her,' Jillian finished firmly. She
paused. 'But you're back now, so surely you can find the
time to do this one small thing for me?'

Patrick felt cornered. 'What do you expect me to do?'

'You know what I expect you to do,' said Jillian reprov-
ingly. 'Get rid of this woman. Do whatever it takes to stop
her seeing Richard. Offer her money if you have to. I've
no doubt half of Rich's attraction is the fact that he's a
director of the company.'

Only Isobel didn't know that. Or, at least, he was fairly
sure she didn't. And he could imagine her reaction if he
offered her money—for anything. For heaven's sake, if she
was already having an affair with Richard—and the idea

still nauseated him—she wouldn't listen to any advice from him. She already suspected his motives for inviting her to have dinner with him. And it wasn't his problem. It wasn't fair of Jillian to load it onto him.

'Leave it with me,' he muttered at last, unwillingly aware of his own involvement in the affair. Because, however he might try to deny it, Isobel had got under his skin, and how could he despise Richard for an attraction that he shared in full measure?

But he wasn't married, he reminded himself tersely. If he were, he might not feel this unwelcome pull of his senses every time Isobel Herriot's name was mentioned. As soon as he was finished with Jillian he'd call Joanna. A night with her would erase the heated emotions that the prospect of seeing Isobel seemed to inspire.

'I love you,' said Jillian fervently, her tears disappearing now that she had got her own way. 'Will you call here on your way back from Horsham? You could spend the night at Kerrymore. You know Mum keeps your room ready.'

'I'll let you know,' said Patrick noncommittally. 'Give Mum my love, won't you?'

'I will.' Jillian had evidently decided not to push her luck. 'See you—soon.'

'Mmm, soon,' agreed Patrick without enthusiasm, and rang off.

He drove out to Horsham the following afternoon.

Instead of letting Joe drive him, he took the powerful little Porsche, running the gauntlet of his chauffeur's objections in doing so.

'What happens if some creep decides to jump you?' Joe had demanded, when the bones of Patrick's intentions had been relayed to him. 'Man! I thought we agreed after the last fiasco that you wouldn't go out alone!'

'Joe, Conrad Martin is behind bars. And the guy was only trying to protect his rights. The council hadn't informed him that they'd sold the land his caravan was pitched on for development.'

'All the same...'

Patrick sighed. 'I'm not completely helpless. I don't need a minder. Not today, at any rate.'

Joe had had to acquiesce, but he wasn't pleased, and Patrick couldn't altogether blame him. Since Conrad Martin had threatened him with a shotgun, he had been forced to take rather more care about his personal safety.

The powerful little sports car ate up the miles between London and Warwickshire. Keeping one eye on the mirror, Patrick allowed the speedometer to creep up. It was good to feel the freedom, good to be driving himself for a change. Apart from the evening when he'd taken Isobel to dinner, he was usually a passenger.

What wasn't so good—or so controllable, for that matter—was the surge of excitement he felt at the thought of seeing Isobel again. He'd had dinner with Joanna the previous evening, with the intention of putting all thoughts of the other woman out of his head. But, although it had been an enjoyable evening, and although he'd accompanied Joanna back to her apartment afterwards, he hadn't gone to bed with her.

And not because she hadn't wanted him to, he remembered grimly. Indeed, he knew she had wanted it, had *expected* it, in fact, and his feeble excuses about the lateness of the hour and overwork had fallen on deaf ears. But the truth was he'd been afraid of making a fool of himself. For when she'd wound her arms around his neck and opened her mouth for his kiss he'd known, for the first time in his life, that he wasn't going to be able to perform.

God! The humiliation he'd felt at that moment had known no bounds. Ever since one of his father's stable-maids had seduced him at the tender age of fourteen, he'd never had any problem in satisfying his partners. It wasn't something he was particularly proud of, but there was no denying that he had begun to take his sexual prowess for granted.

Thankfully, he didn't think Joanna had guessed his secret. Her tight-lipped farewell had owed more to the suspicion that he had found another woman to take her place than to any doubts about his abilities. And there was no other woman, he told himself tersely, refusing to acknowledge that it had been Isobel Herriot's face that had flashed before his eyes when Joanna had attempted to rub herself against him. He was tired, that was all. He was still suffering the after-effects of jetlag. It certainly hadn't been the remembrance of the taste of Isobel's soft lips that had caused his momentary lapse.

The fact remained that if he was having any problems today they were not caused by an absence of potency. On the contrary, he had only to think of himself and Isobel together and an image of her naked and writhing beneath him on a bed filled his vision. Dammit, he could get hard just picturing her round butt, or those breasts, which simply cried out for him to fill his hands with them. And not just his hands, he appended, forcing back the urge to press down on the accelerator. He wanted to kiss them, and stroke them, and suck on those provocative nipples. Who was he kidding? *He wanted her.* And he wouldn't have a minute's peace until he'd had her.

By the time he reached the outskirts of Horsham-on-the-Water, he had himself in control again. He parked the car in a designated parking space, paid the fee, and attached the ticket to the windscreen. He had no desire to be in trouble with the law, even if parking fines in London had become a way of life.

He came out onto the high street about a dozen yards and a road's width from the craft shop. It enabled him to view his destination without arousing attention, and he considered going into a nearby bar and getting himself a beer before tackling the interview.

He still wasn't precisely sure what he should say to her. The idea of admitting that he was related to Richard did not appeal to him at all. Nor did the idea of giving her notice, even though Jillian was right—with the renewal of the leases coming up, he had the ideal opportunity to hand. What Richard would say if he told him what he planned to do didn't concern him. Just at the moment his brother-in-law's feelings were the least of his worries.

The shop was closed!

He saw the sign as soon as he crossed the road. Because shops didn't draw their blinds these days for security reasons, and it was a fairly bright afternoon, he hadn't noticed before that the lights weren't on inside. But now he could see that despite the fact that all its fellows were doing a roaring trade Caprice was very definitely locked up.

His brow furrowing, he looked about him. He supposed he could go into the café next door and ask the staff if they knew where Isobel was, but he was loath to advertise his presence to all and sundry. There was always the possibility that someone might have seen his picture in a newspaper or a news magazine, and until he chose to tell Isobel who he was he preferred to keep his real identity to himself.

He sighed and glanced at his watch. It was a quarter to four. Too late for her to be out for lunch, but perhaps not too late for a mid-afternoon break. But would she take a break and close the shop? If she didn't have any assistance today, she might have to. But somehow, knowing what he did of Isobel, he doubted it. She seemed far too conscientious to neglect her customers.

One thing was certain—it wasn't half-day closing. A glance at the times of opening pinned to the door revealed that the shop was open every day but Sunday from nine in the morning until six in the evening. It didn't always close for lunch, he knew. So something must have happened for the shop to be shut today.

Had she and Richard gone away together?

The thought shook his hard-won self-control, and for a moment his hands clenched, imitating what he'd like to do to Richard's neck if it were so. Was his brother-in-law reckless enough to risk everything for sex? he wondered savagely. He didn't credit him with loving Isobel. Richard loved no one but himself.

He took a deep breath and forced himself to relax. He was jumping to conclusions. Just because the shop was closed that was no reason to put the blame on Rich. She could be away; she could be on holiday; she could even be sick! She hadn't known he was coming, and even if she had

he doubted she'd have changed her arrangements to ac-
commodate him.

He was walking back to where he had parked the car,
speculating on the advisability of calling at the cottage, when
someone said, 'Hello.' It was the assistant, Chris, the one
who'd given him Isobel's address. She was smiling, so there
couldn't be anything wrong, could there? He pushed his
hands into his trouser pockets. There was only one way to
find out.

'Not working today?' he asked, despising the banality of
his question, but Chris was obviously not put out.

'Issy's had to close the shop for a few days,' she explained. 'Her mother fell and broke her ankle at the
weekend and Issy's having to look after her until she's able
to get about again.'

'I see.' Patrick didn't know whether to feel glad or sorry.
He was relieved that his worst fears had not been realised,
of course, but he could hardly go and see her at her parents'
house, not when he didn't have a convincing reason for
doing so.

'Did you want to see her?'

Chris was nothing if not candid, and Patrick weighed the
potential advantages of admitting that he did against the
drawback of arousing her curiosity. 'Perhaps,' he said, acknowledging the word for the equivocation it was. 'I
suppose she's staying with her parents. Do you have any
idea when she's coming back to work?'

'She's not staying with her parents,' declared the girl at
once. 'She just spends the day there. Once her father fin-
ishes surgery, she comes home. She gets back to the cottage
at about seven o'clock.'

Patrick inclined his head. 'OK. Thanks.' So Isobel's
father was a doctor, was he? That was something he hadn't
known before. He felt a certain amount of complicity in
questioning her assistant, but his curiosity was equally as
sharp as hers—at least where her employer was concerned.

'Are you staying in Horsham?'

She evidently felt that her assistance warranted a certain
amount of feedback, but Patrick was not in the habit of

confiding his affairs to anyone. 'Thanks again for your help,' he said instead, putting a couple of strides between them. He lifted a hand in farewell. 'Good bye.'

Sitting in his car some minutes later, he brooded over what she had told him. If Isobel was not expected to return to her cottage until seven o'clock that evening, it looked as if he had had a wasted journey. He'd phoned his mother before he'd left for Horsham and promised her he'd join her for dinner. If he hung around until seven o'clock, it could be nine o'clock before he got to Kerrymore. It wouldn't be fair to let her down even if his motives were supposed to be selfless.

Of course his reasons for phoning his mother in the first place had been less so. He'd deliberately made the arrangement to ensure that he had an excuse for getting away. Not that he'd flattered himself that Isobel might try and prevent him. He didn't trust himself, that was the truth.

He scowled. All this for a woman who was having an affair with a married man. It was just as well Richard wasn't around at the moment. Patrick doubted his ability to be discreet. But Richard was in Holland, sent there on a week's assignment this morning. He'd grumbled, but he'd had no choice in the matter, and Patrick had known an unwarranted sense of shame at his own deceit.

But no longer. Here he was, with at least three hours to fill before Isobel was even available, and the knowledge that he was expected in Oxford by eight o'clock. Dammit, he didn't have a choice. He'd have to come back tomorrow. He couldn't let his mother down. It really wouldn't be fair...

CHAPTER SEVEN

ISOBEL drove back to the cottage feeling justifiably miffed. She had spent the whole day pandering to her mother's frustration, only to have her father come home at half past six and accuse her of wasting her time. The woman—her mother—was impossible, he'd declared. It wasn't his—or Isobel's—fault that she had been reckless enough to balance on a chair that wasn't safe, it wasn't their fault she had had this accident, and she should stop blaming them for her own ineptitude.

Of course, this remark had resulted in another of her parents' increasingly frequent arguments, and although Isobel was fairly sure they would emerge unscathed from the conflict she wasn't sure she would. As usual when the accusations were flagging, she herself had become the object of their resentment, and remarks to the effect that if she was married she wouldn't have time to run a business and no one had asked her to close the shop in the height of the season had constituted a united attack.

The upshot of it was that Isobel had left before she had felt compelled to make some accusations of her own. It wasn't fair of them to involve her in their arguments, and although her mother was gradually managing to get about on her cast the first couple of days she had been wearing the thing had proved traumatic. Besides, Isobel would have liked to ask her father who he thought would have made the meals if she hadn't chipped in. Her mother was not a homebody at the best of times, and although she got by, buying ready-made meals from Marks & Spencer, she had not had the opportunity to go shopping since the accident.

In consequence, Isobel was in no mood to be tolerant when she turned into the lane and found another car blocking her gate. It was bad enough that she had had to manoeuvre her way though rows of parked cars at lunchtime, but now it was after seven o'clock; all the visitors should have gone.

It wasn't until she had parked her little Peugeot as close to the car in front as possible that she realised someone was sitting in it. It was a low-slung Porsche, with tinted windows, so it was not surprising that she hadn't noticed the driver before. Besides, why would anyone be sitting in a Porsche at her gate? It wasn't Richard, unless he'd changed his car.

Then who...?

The thought—and a possible explanation—had barely formed in her mind when the door of the Porsche was thrust open from the inside and a man got out. And not just any man: it was Patrick Riker. Dear God, she thought, what was he doing here? After the way she'd treated him last time she'd seen him, she'd been sure he wouldn't come back.

Except for that kiss...

But it hadn't been a real kiss, she assured herself, making no effort to get out of her car. And although he had asked if he could give her a ring next time he was in the area she had thought that was a courtesy thing at best. She'd been rude; she'd practically accused him of having some ulterior motive for trying to manipulate her, when, taken at its face value, his offer should have been attractive. Horsham was, after all, something of a backwater, whatever passing trade it did attract.

She swallowed, watching him as he closed the car door and strolled towards her. It was the first time she'd seen him in anything other than a suit, and she was alarmed by the way her eyes were drawn to his lean, muscular body. He was wearing a black knit shirt, open at the collar, to expose the strong brown column of his throat, and close-fitting black trousers, made of some supple fabric, which moulded every contour of his legs.

Oh, God...

She felt a beading of perspiration on her upper lip that had nothing to do with the humidity either inside or outside the car. And, realising that any minute he was going to reach the car and possibly rest his elbows on the open window as he spoke to her, thus bringing his face within a few inches of her own, she hurriedly closed the windows, opened the door and stumbled out.

'Hello.'

His greeting was friendly enough, and Isobel wondered if she'd been exaggerating the importance of her response to his offer. Just because she wasn't used to having one-on-one dealings with men like him, there was no reason to suppose he shared her embarrassment. She was fairly sure he didn't. In fact, she decided, feeding the resentment her parents had kindled, she was fairly sure that nothing she did could embarrass him.

'Hello.'

Her reply was terse, and she saw the way his lips tightened at the unspoken reproof. He must know he wasn't welcome, she thought. And if he imagined she might have changed her mind he was mistaken. She had no intention of entering another rat race. One experience was quite enough.

'I was sorry to hear about your mother,' he remarked as she locked her car, and she reminded herself to give Chris a piece of her mind when she saw her. She had no right to be gossiping about her affairs to all and sundry. The girl knew nothing about Patrick Riker, except what Isobel herself had told her. And that had been precious little, despite her being accused of being mean.

'Thank you,' she responded now, putting the car keys into her haversack and starting along the pavement. 'I assume you've been speaking to my assistant? Tell me, is that how you get all your information? From gossip?'

Patrick's dark brows descended. 'What the hell is that supposed to mean?'

'Just what you think it means,' retorted Isobel curtly, opening her gate and turning to close it behind her. But Patrick was right behind her, so there was no way she could bar his entrance, and her next retort died on her lips at the sight of the darkening scowl on his face.

'I saw...Chris—is that her name?—in the high street, sure,' he told her harshly. 'And she told me why the shop was closed. I didn't know it was a state secret. You should have put a sign to that effect in the window.'

Isobel bent her head, ostensibly looking for her house keys. 'It's not a state secret,' she said tightly. 'I just don't like you questioning my employees behind my back.'

'Your employees?' he echoed. 'How many *employees* do you have? I must have missed them.'

Isobel pressed her lips together for a moment. 'All right, I only have one employee, but that doesn't matter. I can't imagine why you needed the information. I thought we'd said all there was to say weeks ago.'

'Weeks ago?' He regarded her with cool green eyes. 'It's not that long since I was last in Horsham, and I don't recall telling you why I'm here this evening.'

'But you went to the shop,' she pointed out, albeit a little doubtfully now. 'If you'd wanted to get in touch with me, you could have phoned.'

Patrick's mouth compressed. 'Yes, I could,' he agreed, and she wondered if she had only imagined the strange look that had crossed his face as he'd spoken. 'But perhaps I was just in the district; perhaps I thought of looking you up on the spur of the moment.' He paused. 'Or perhaps I wanted to speak to you—personally. Why don't you invite me in and find out?'

Isobel caught her breath. 'I—I can't.'

'Why can't you?'

'I—have other plans.'

Yeah, right. A shower, a glass of wine, and supper for one.

Patrick frowned. 'So you won't even offer me a cup of coffee? The one I turned down ten days ago?'

Isobel licked her dry lips. 'Why are you here, Mr Riker?'

'Patrick,' he said at once. 'My name's Patrick. And, believe it or not, I don't really know. I was supposed to be having dinner with my mother this evening. But it suddenly seemed more—important to see you.'

Isobel felt the colour pour into her face. 'Mr Riker—'

'Patrick. Or Pat, if you'd rather.'

'—I think you're making a fool of me—'

'No!'

'Yes.' Isobel put her key in the door. 'Stop pretending. I know you're not interested in me. Men like you—well, men of your... background,' she amended awkwardly, 'do not get involved with frumpish spinsters with attitude. I'm sure you think it's amusing to play these games, but I know there's something more to it than that.'

'That's not true.'

'What's not true?'

'That—that you're a frumpish spinster,' he told her impatiently. 'What do you want me to say? That you're a very sexy lady? That any man would be proud to think you were interested in him—?'

'I don't want you to say anything,' she exploded hotly, sure now that he was just playing a game. 'Go away, Mr Riker; I'm not interested. Not in you, not in your proposition, and certainly not in your lies!'

The key turned and the door opened and she almost fell into the hallway in her haste to get away, but she wasn't quick enough. Patrick Riker's foot was on the threshold, and unless he removed it she hadn't a hope in hell of closing the door.

'For God's sake,' he said, and she could tell by the lights glinting in his eyes that he was angry now. 'Are you crazy? I come here with the best of intentions and all you can do is throw a spit!'

'Well, that's what spinsters do,' retorted Isobel painfully, aware that her knees were trembling beneath her long skirt. 'Will you please get your foot out of my doorway? I'm not in the mood to have a fight.'

'I'd say that was exactly what you were in the mood for,' declared Patrick grimly, forcing the door open against her will and stepping into the dark hallway. 'Now, stop behaving as if you're afraid I'm going to jump you. It doesn't quite jell with the disparaging opinion you're supposed to have of yourself.'

'How dare you—?'

'What? Have an alternative opinion? Believe me, Isobel, if I'd planned to seduce you, I'd have chosen a location that was familiar to me, not you.'

Isobel's breath left her lungs in a rush, and then, re-alising she was unlikely to be able to eject him without his cooperation, she allowed her shoulders to sag. What was she getting so het up about? she wondered frustratedly. Whatever his faults, she doubted he'd ever had to force a woman to have sex with him in his life. Whether she could trust him was another story. But, if she kept her head, she'd soon find out what he really wanted.

With a squaring of her shoulders, she opened the door to the living room, allowing an orange shaft of sunlight to dispel the shadows in the hall. But the pleasant smell of pot-pourri couldn't quite disguise the male scent of Patrick Riker's body behind her, and she knew it would take more than opening all the windows to erase his presence even after he'd gone.

Politeness came to the rescue. 'Tea?' she offered tightly, dropping her haversack and stepping into her small kitchen. 'I'm afraid I can't offer you a beer. I only keep wine in the house.'

'Wine would be very nice,' he accepted, despite the fact that that wasn't what she'd offered, and Isobel contained her annoyance as she extracted the bottle of Niersteiner from the fridge. She'd been looking forward to opening it after she'd had her shower, and there was a bowl of salad already made to go with a slice of asparagus quiche.

When she stepped back into the living room, Patrick was standing by her bureau, examining the photographs of her brother and sister-in-law and their children which occupied a central position. 'Not yours, I assume,' he said as she handed him a glass of wine, indicating the picture of her nephew and niece, and Isobel wished she could disconcert him by saying that they were.

'My brother's,' she replied shortly, gesturing towards an armchair. 'Why don't you sit down, Mr Riker? Make yourself comfortable.'

His lips took on a knowing slant. 'Is that what you really want me to do?' he asked, and Isobel felt a sudden wave of heat sweep up her cheeks. What did she really want? she wondered unsteadily, not unaware of his attraction, despite her indignation. It was easier to dismiss his charm when he wasn't so close.

'What I want is for you to go,' she declared at last, not wholly convincingly, but she was relieved nevertheless when he lowered his weight into a chintz-covered armchair. She didn't like him prowling about her possessions, or asking questions about her personal life. 'I haven't changed my mind about the shop, nor am I likely to do so.'

He frowned down at the glass of wine in his hand. 'As a matter of fact, I didn't come here to discuss the shop,' he said at last, surprising her. He lifted his head. 'I wanted to see you again. Purely for my own pleasure.'

Isobel caught her breath. 'You're not serious!'

'Why not?' His eyes narrowed. 'Do you have a problem with that?'

Isobel gave a somewhat dazed shake of her head. 'I don't believe you.'

Patrick's brows arched. 'There's someone else?'

'No—that is—' Isobel supposed she could pretend that Richard was her boyfriend. He would like to be; that was becoming increasingly obvious. The only thing was, she was no more interested in him than she had been in any of her other would-be admirers. 'I—that's my business,' she finished tersely.

'So there is someone else.' Was it her imagination, or did his face suddenly look more severe? she wondered. It couldn't be that he was jealous. My God, if it wasn't so unlikely it would be laughable.

Isobel turned away. She hadn't brought herself a glass of wine, hoping to convey the impression that his visit was to be deliberately short-lived. But now she wished she had. Anything to give her hands some occupation.

'I don't think it's any business of yours,' she declared at last, pretending to study the print of the Rialto Bridge that hung over the screened fireplace. 'I'm sorry if you've had a wasted journey. But if that's all you have to say I think—'

'It's not.' The warmth of his breath on her neck startled her, and she half turned to find that he had left his seat and come to stand right behind her. 'Tell me—tell me about this other man. Is the relationship serious or not?'

Isobel forced herself to meet his eyes. She didn't know why it was so hard all of a sudden, but she had to nip this particular shoot in the bud. She wasn't interested in a relationship, particularly not with a man who was probably just looking for kicks. And one-night stands were not her forte either, whatever her appearance might have led him to believe.

'It's serious,' she said, not knowing she was actually going to say that until the words were out. But he was so close, she could see the fine network of lines around his eyes— eyes that were disturbingly sensual, and far too knowing for comfort.

'Is it?' Was that disbelief in his tone? Disappointment? Disapproval? 'Who is he? Tell me his name. You never know, I might have met him.'

'You?' Isobel swallowed, glad of the incredulity, that helped to dispel the sudden intimacy between them. 'I don't think that's very likely. He doesn't move in the kind of circles you do.'

Patrick set his now empty glass down on the mantelshelf. 'What kind of circles would those be?' he enquired, allowing his fingers to trail almost suggestively down its stem. 'You don't know anything about me. Unless you've been checking up on me without my knowledge.'

'You wish!' Isobel's response was automatic, and to hide her sudden embarrassment she added tautly, 'You have a chauffeur; you drive a Rolls-Royce—'

'A Bentley, actually.'

'Well . . .' She licked her lips. 'Richard drives a Vauxhall.' Damn, she hadn't intended to mention any names. 'He— he's just an ordinary—salesman.' There; he couldn't make any connection from that.

Patrick frowned. 'He told you he was a salesman?'

'Yes.' Isobel blinked. 'What are you implying? That he was lying to me?'

'Of course not.' His denial was almost too pat. 'Um—have you known him long?'

'Long enough.' Isobel held up her head defiantly. 'And that's all the questions I intend to answer.' She took a breath. 'I think you ought to go.'

Patrick's eyes darkened. 'You're seeing him tonight?'

'No! *Yes!*' Isobel was angry with herself for feeling the need to lie. For God's sake, she didn't owe this man anything. She wished now that she'd stayed with her parents in spite of their animosity.

'I don't believe you.'

He meant it. She could tell that by the sudden easing of his mood. The tension was unwinding from his body, and his stance became looser and less aggressive.

'It's true,' she protested, compounding her duplicity, only to see his lips curl into a mocking smile. How did he know she was lying? she wondered. Was she so transparent? Or didn't he care, one way or the other?

'OK,' he acknowledged, and then, when she could have stepped away from him, he lifted his hand and cupped the nape of her neck. 'You smell nice,' he said as disbelief that she was allowing this to happen and weakness at the sensuality of his touch warred within her. 'You don't really want to send me away, do you?'

Isobel gulped. For a moment, for a brief, heart-stopping moment, she wanted to say no, but common sense—and a belated awareness of her own vulnerability where this man was concerned—came to her rescue. 'Yes,' she said, and then more firmly, 'Yes—yes, I do. I'm sorry to disappoint you, but I don't do this sort of thing.'

'What sort of thing?'

He was being deliberately obtuse, and she was tempted not to expand on her explanation. But his eyes were roaming her face with unnerving penetration, and she actually felt as if it was a physical exploration, and one which might become a reality if she didn't put a stop to it at once.

'This sort of thing,' she informed him stiffly, attempting to step back to dislodge his hand. 'I'm not interested in you, Mr Riker. However hard you may find that to believe.'

'Because of this man you're involved with?' he prompted, and she caught her breath.

'I don't propose to answer that. I want you to leave.'

'Well, you're not opposed to sex,' he continued, as if she hadn't spoken. 'You've been having an affair with this man Richard, after all.'

'How dare you?' Isobel was aghast. 'You know nothing about my relationship with—with Richard.'

'But you do have one,' he declared softly. 'You said so.'

'I also said that I wanted you to leave,' said Isobel, annoyed to find that her voice was slightly unsteady. 'You have no right to take advantage of your position.'

'And what position would that be?' he persisted, his thumb stroking the smooth column of her throat, as if that was all that interested him. 'You're a very sensuous woman, Miss Herriot. Has Richard told you that?'

Isobel drew a breath. 'Leave Richard out of this.'

'Oh, I'm quite prepared to,' agreed Patrick Riker gently. 'So long as you do the same,' he added softly, and bent his head and covered her mouth with his.

CHAPTER EIGHT

HE SHOULDN'T have touched her.

As soon as Patrick's mouth brushed hers, he knew he was playing a dangerous game. Oh, he'd kissed her before, lightly, briefly, an automatic end to the evening they had spent together, but that hadn't even stirred his senses. Well, only slightly, he admitted wryly. But nothing he couldn't handle.

This was different. He knew that the moment he felt Isobel's lips quivering beneath his own. He'd thought she was playing a game, but she wasn't. Whatever the relationship was that she had with Richard, she was not the seasoned temptress he had imagined.

And despite knowing that she really did want him to go before anything untoward happened he found himself incapable of obeying his better instincts. For some reason, the fresh taste of her mouth, the clean scent of her breath were more intoxicating than the wine she'd offered so reluctantly earlier. Not that her lips were any less reluctant, he realised ruefully. For all he was being aroused by the tenderness of her mouth, he sensed that her participation was unwilling. She was pressing her lips together as if her life depended on it, and her hands were balled into resistant fists against his chest.

But he couldn't let her go. Not without making her respond to him even marginally. He wanted her to part her lips, to open her mouth and let him slide his tongue into its hot, moist interior. He wanted her to kiss him back with all the passion of which he was sure she was capable.

Ignoring the caution that had protected him through years of self-preservation, Patrick brought his other hand up to cup her face between his palms. 'Sweet,' he said huskily, rubbing his lips back and forth across hers. 'Come on, Belle, stop fighting me. We both know that's not what you want to do.'

Her expression was mutinous, but she was not foolish enough to try and answer him. To do so would entail opening her mouth, and she seemed determined to keep him at bay.

Let her go!

The voice of his conscience rose above the heated roar of his senses, but he pushed it away. It wasn't as if he intended her any harm, he told himself impatiently in defence of his actions. He just wanted to find out how experienced she really was, understand for himself what Richard saw in her.

But he thought he already knew. There was something intensely feminine about her, something more than the intelligence in her face and the allure of her slim, lissom body. Which wasn't so slim in parts, he acknowledged, aware of the taut swell of her breasts pushing against the thin cotton of her shirt. She had an attraction that was more than mere physical beauty, and which gave her an appeal that he found almost irresistible.

Almost?

He slid his hands into her hair, feeling the thick strands curling about his fingers. Then, giving in to the almost overwhelming urge he was experiencing, he covered her face and eyelids with hot kisses, avoiding looking into those golden eyes that watched him with such distrust.

And slowly but surely he felt her resistance weakening. Slowly but surely her eyes closed, as if she couldn't bear to face the truth of her submission. With an almost imperceptible shudder, she swayed against him, and the warm swell of her breasts pressed against his chest.

The feeling was incredible. He'd never experienced such an instantaneous response within himself before. He wanted to crush her even closer, to take her in his arms and bury himself inside her. The heat of his arousal was almost painful as she pressed herself against him and it was all he could do to retain his sanity.

She smelled so sweet. The warmth of her body was like a potent intoxicant, mingling as it did the scents of the delicate perfume she was wearing and her soft skin. His senses were filled with her sensuous allure, his nerve-endings tingling with the awareness of what he wanted to do.

His breathing faltered as his tongue stroked the line where her lips joined. The seam they'd created seemed less tightly blended now, her lips trembling slightly beneath his probing caress.

And then they parted. He wasn't sure whether it happened because she wanted it to happen, or because she'd been forced to take a breath. Whatever, her breath escaped to fan his burning senses, and with a feeling almost of recognition his tongue slid into her mouth.

At that moment, all thought of restraint was banished. He could no more have drawn back then than have prevented night from following day. His whole being was engulfed in a sensation that left all previous experiences far behind, and, giving in to an irresistible impulse, he wrapped his arms about her.

She felt absurdly vulnerable. For such a tall young woman she felt almost delicate, and distinctly frail. No, not frail, fragile, he corrected himself swiftly. She inspired an unwilling feeling of protectiveness inside him, a reluctant knowledge that whatever happened here he would be to blame for it.

But the reservations that such an awareness generated were quickly eliminated. Although his brain was still functioning, his desire was fast outstripping any feelings of conscience he might have. Intellectually, he might despise what he was doing, but for once his physical needs were uppermost. The woman who had scarcely been out of his thoughts since the first time he'd seen her was in his arms, and he was not about to lose that advantage.

She didn't resist him. Indeed, as his possession of her mouth grew more urgent, more passionate, he sensed the battle she was having with herself not to respond. He couldn't be absolutely sure, but he suspected that the tentative stroke of her tongue against his was not wholly accidental, and when she uttered a helpless little moan he was sure.

His hands moved lower, sliding over the slim blades of her shoulders to the slender curve of her waist. And as he caressed her he felt the shuddering waves of awareness that swept over her, so that when his hands settled on her hips, and he brought her fully against his engorged body, it was hard to think of anything but that.

She seemed to think so too, because the hands that had been obstructing his advance now relaxed and rested weakly against his chest. One nail snagged the open neckline of his shirt almost possessively, and he was amazed at the hot reaction it inspired.

'God,' he groaned as her mouth opened wider and he bit softly on the inner curve of her lip. She tasted so good, every bit as good as he had anticipated, and when she gave a little gulp and wound her arms around his neck his head swam with the urgent demands of the flesh.

He wanted to touch her, and one hand came up, almost of its own accord, to invade the open neckline of *her* shirt. The skin of her neck and shoulder was like the softest silk beneath his exploring fingers, and she caught her breath when he unfastened several more buttons and exposed the upper slopes of her breasts.

'You're beautiful,' he breathed huskily, aware that this time he meant the words he had spoken so many times before. She was beautiful—beautiful and responsive and sexy—and for the first time in his life he was as much at the mercy of his senses as she was.

'Patrick...'

His name on her lips was a mixture of denial and protest. He knew that although she had given in to the needs he had aroused inside her she was still wary of committing herself to a man she barely knew.

'Isobel,' he said by way of response, his fingertips seeking and finding the crested peaks beneath the fabric of her shirt. 'Do you mind?' he asked, but it wasn't really a question. He was already bending his head to suckle her through the cloth.

Her reaction was unexpected. Instead of enjoying the sensation, she dug her nails into his shoulders and said, 'Oh, God, oh, God, oh, God,' in a breathless, excited voice, almost as if she'd never experienced such a thing before.

Well, perhaps Richard wasn't quite the stud he thought he was, mused Patrick disparagingly, momentarily remembering what had brought him here. But it was a fleeting thought—one that was soon buried beneath the needs of the moment. Besides, he didn't want to think about Richard; he didn't want to contemplate the fact that his brother-in-law had already enjoyed the intimacies he was presently sharing with Isobel, and his reaction was to tear the remaining buttons apart and expose the upper half of her body to his hungry gaze.

He had shocked her; he could see that in the depths of those golden eyes, and as if the cool air assaulting her body had cooled her blood she dragged herself away from him and turned her back.

'Please—' she said, and he could tell that the word was dragged from her lips. 'I want you to go.'

Are you kidding?

Had he said that? Or had he only thought it? The latter, it seemed, because she didn't respond, and, gathering his senses, he stepped close behind her. Sliding his arms about her waist, he brought her back against him, and bent his head to touch her nape with his tongue.

'You don't mean that.'

'I did—I do—' But she lifted one shoulder as if to facilitate his caress, and his hands closed possessively over her breasts.

'No, you don't,' he breathed as she shivered and tilted her head back against his shoulder. He nuzzled her ear. 'Do you?'

She swallowed. 'I—no. No!' she confessed, turning round in his arms, and, winding her arms about his neck, she lifted her face to his.

There was no turning back. Patrick knew that the moment she surrendered to his possession of her mouth. She was no longer an unwilling participant; she was every inch his equal, sharing his hunger, meeting his passion, and just as eager as he was to satisfy her needs. Indeed, although he had suspected that she had hidden depths, even he had had no conception of how responsive she would be—or how desirable, he conceded, acknowledging what he had only suspected earlier—that she was everything he had ever wanted in a woman.

And although some lingering thread of reason warned him against what he was about to do he couldn't seem to stop himself. Abandoning any thought of leaving her, he cupped her face between his hands and ran his thumbs across her yielding lips. 'Let's go upstairs,' he said, his voice suddenly thick and urgent, and without another word she led him out of the room . . .

Some time later—he didn't know how long it was; perhaps an hour, perhaps only half that time—Patrick lay on his back staring grimly at the slightly uneven slope of Isobel's bedroom ceiling. He looked relaxed, but he didn't feel it. Even though he'd just indulged in the best sex he'd ever known, the satiation of his body was in direct opposition to the frantic turmoil of his thoughts.

Hell!

The oath he silently uttered was powerful, but not powerful enough. He felt as if no words he used could ever remove the sense of remorse he was experiencing. In addition to that he was angry—angry and depressed and bitterly frustrated at the immature way he'd behaved.

Hell!

He used the word again, in an effort to make sense of the desperate way he was feeling. But his thoughts were all pessimistic, the results of his recklessness past dispute.

How had it happened?

But that was a stupid question, not worthy of an answer. He knew only too well how it had happened. Even now, racked by the kind of guilt he hadn't known since he was an adolescent, just the thought of her had the power to turn him on. Lying here beside her, in her bedroom, in her *bed*, smelling the sweet-sour scent of her sweat, knowing he was responsible for the exhausted sleep she was now enjoying were all potent aphrodisiacs as far as he was concerned.

He didn't even have to look at her. He already had the image of her imprinted on his brain. She was lying on her stomach, totally nude and totally uninhibited. Though he guessed she might not be quite so wonderfully abandoned when she awoke.

Dear God!

He didn't want to anticipate what might happen when she did wake up. Actually, he thought, if he had any sense, he'd make his escape now, while he could. But there would be something so cowardly about leaving her without any explanation. Though what explanation she would accept he didn't know. The truth was, there was no explanation; it had been just a terrible misunderstanding. He'd made love to his brother-in-law's mistress—only to find she wasn't.

He closed his eyes for a moment, and then stared at the ceiling again, as if he might find inspiration among the nooks and crannies of its sloping eaves. Towards the open sash windows the ceiling lowered, creating two matching alcoves, and pretty flowered curtains blew in the breeze.

It was a pretty room, he reflected, trying to be objective. The bed was a genuine four-poster, and spread with one of the hand-sewn quilts Isobel sold at the craft shop. The predominant colours of peach and green matched the billowing curtains, and the soft cream carpet underfoot accentuated its feminine appeal.

She stirred, and, against his will, he turned to look at her. But all she did was burrow more deeply into the pillows, cradling her head on one arm and exposing one rose-tipped breast to his gaze.

God!

The urge to touch her was almost irresistible. He felt himself hardening in spite of himself, felt the need to fill his mouth with her sweetness overwhelming his reason. He had only to stretch out his hand, cup that provocative bottom, and part the delicious cleft with his fingers ...

He jerked his head around, forcing himself to look away from her. His body protested, the ache between his thighs developing into a real physical pain, but he fought against seeking any relief. He had to think; he had to put what had happened into perspective. And—he lifted a languid wrist and glanced at his watch—he had to phone his mother. He was already going to be too late for supper, even if it was still light beyond those ancient window-frames.

Supper!

The banality of the thought appalled him. As if it mattered whether he was late for supper or not. Of course, he regretted disappointing his mother; of course, he owed it to her to tell her where he was so she wouldn't worry. But he couldn't tell her what he had been doing. Couldn't tell Jillian either, he mused bitterly. Especially not her.

And yet...

And yet when he'd invited Isobel to take him upstairs he'd been so confident that he knew what he was doing. Oh, he'd had his doubts—what man wouldn't, given the circumstances?—but it hadn't seemed like a life-or-death decision. She was Richard's 'bit on the side', the woman his brother-in-law was having an affair with, the woman who was breaking his sister's heart without any apparrent consciousness of the fact.

Only she wasn't.

He closed his eyes as the memory of what had happened filled his vision: the memory of how he had held her, and undressed her, and encouraged her to undress him. Beneath her loose shirt and baggy skirt he had discovered a body to die for: slim, as he'd already expected, but rounded too, with the generous breasts he had already seen, and with long, shapely legs. Her hips were wider than Joanna's, but perfectly proportioned, her thighs strong and muscular, her calves taut and firm. In short, she did herself no favours by dressing like some latter-day hippie. Without those ugly boots her feet were slender, her ankles more than just an extension of her legs.

She had seemed nervous, he remembered now, though at the time he'd put it down to a natural reserve. After all, although he was prepared to believe that she and Richard were an item, he was not of the opinion that she spread herself around. He was even willing to accept that she didn't make a habit of going to bed with all her boyfriends. There was something too fastidious about her for that.

Which might have been why he'd lost his head as he had, he reflected unhappily. He wasn't in the habit of sleeping around either—at least, not since he was a boy. There'd been women, of course there had, but he wasn't a natural predator. His mother and his sister had taught him to have respect for their sex, and he was basically a decent man.

Or he'd thought he was until today, he mused bitterly. Although, remembering Isobel's fingers unfastening his buttons, loosening his belt, surrounding the throbbing length of his manhood, he couldn't blame himself entirely for what he'd done. He hadn't known a woman more responsive, hadn't realised that an instinctual curiosity was all it was.

Had he been so wrapped up in his own selfish needs that he hadn't recognised the signs sooner? Or—God forgive him!—had he begun to suspect the truth long before he'd eased himself into her body? Would he have stopped—could he have stopped—if the proof had been presented sooner? Or would he have made love to her anyway, knowing that only she could satisfy his need?

Whatever the truth of it was, Isobel had not tried to stop him. Indeed, remembering how she had writhed beneath him, he found it hard, even now, to see what else he could have done. He was only human, after all, and she had been so eager...

But it was his fault—his fault for using the not inconsiderable skills he possessed to arouse her to such a state of excitement that she couldn't deny him. She had been desperate for him to take her—and he had.

He remembered well his swimming senses, and the urgency he'd felt to lose himself in her. She'd been moist and tight, and only faintly apprehensive, and it had not been until he'd surged through that fragile barrier that he'd realised the truth.

She had been a virgin!

He swallowed. Of course, it had been too late then. In more ways than one. He wasn't in the habit of carrying protection with him, and he'd consoled himself with the thought that if she was having an affair with Richard she must be on the Pill. Not that that was any excuse, he knew. The dangers of sexually transmitted diseases were always present. But he'd wanted nothing to interrupt them; he'd wanted to make love to her, skin to skin.

And the awareness of that reality, of her tight muscles contracting about his in perfect harmony, had forced him over the brink. Before he could even think about withdrawing—even had he found the strength to do so—the inevitable had happened, and his seed had spurted into her womb with satisfying heat. God! He could still feel the slick warmth of her around him, the aftermath of his orgasm leaving him shuddering in her arms.

It couldn't have been a very satisfying experience for her, he thought self-disparagingly, even though she had neither blamed him nor reproached him for what he'd done. And, like any selfish brute, he'd fallen asleep on her, only awakening when it was too late to make amends.

He stifled a groan. He should leave. He ought to leave. He was serving no good purpose by staying here. She might even resent what had happened when she woke up. Who could blame her? He was a bastard of the first order.

But still he stayed, watching the sky outside turn from blue to gold. It never got completely dark until much later at this time of the year. He guessed it must be about nine o'clock, and to confirm it he put out his hand and turned on the bedside lamp.

Isobel opened her eyes. His movements, combined with the sudden illumination, had disturbed her, and she blinked at him in some confusion, belatedly becoming aware of her state of undress.

'Oh!'

Her embarrassment was endearing, and despite the disgust he had felt with himself for his earlier behaviour he found himself rolling towards her and preventing her from drawing the crumpled sheet about her.

'Hi,' he said huskily, stroking a caressing hand across her hot cheek. 'Sleepyhead!'

'Didn't you—? I mean—I thought—I must have been more tired than I imagined.'

'Now, how am I supposed to answer that?' he teased, drawing a honey-gold strand of hair through his fingers.

'You aren't.'

Her eyes darkened, and, realising he had to say something—*do* something—to assuage his guilt, he sighed. 'I'm sorry.'

'Oh, I—don't be.'

Her consternation was evident, and he wondered, not for the first time, how she had managed to go so long without some man suspecting what lay beneath that modest exterior.

'But I am,' he insisted, cupping her cheek with one hand and smoothing his thumb over the faint shadow that lay beneath her eye. 'I had no idea.'

'Why should you have?' Her response was taut and jerky. 'I suppose I should have—warned you. I just didn't—'

'Don't say any more, or I'll feel even worse than I already do,' he told her gently, and she frowned.

'Why should you feel bad? Oh—' She moistened lips that were already soft and bruised from his lovemaking. 'Was it—painful—?'

'No.' His denial verged on impatient, and, ignoring the warning voices that were already clamouring in his head, he bent his head and covered her mouth with his own. 'You were sweet, and quite unforgettable. I'm just sorry it was such a disappointment for you.'

'It wasn't,' she protested, framing his face now with her hands and studying him with unnerving clarity. 'I've wondered—often—what it would be like. It had to be someone, and I'm glad it was you.'

Patrick expelled a rueful breath. 'But you didn't—' He broke off. 'It all happened far too fast for you to enjoy it. Believe me, I'm not usually so selfish. But you—well, I'm afraid I lost my head.'

'I'm glad.' Her smile was diffident. 'I did, too. I don't make a habit of this either.'

'I know.' The admission was heartfelt, the guilt he was feeling rearing its head again. 'But believe me, you were...beautiful.' He paused. 'I don't want to let you go.'

It was the truth, but he had no right to say it, particularly as her response to that was to turn more fully towards him. Now her full round breasts teased the light covering of hair that marked his pectorals, the careless brush of her thighs unbearably sensual against the coarse hair that cradled his sex.

And, against all sense of reason, his body responded instantly to the touch of hers. She was aware of it, too, snatching in a gulp of air in response to the feel of his heavy arousal against her stomach. Not that she objected; as if it was the most natural thing on earth, her soft lips curved in a purely sensuous smile. With a sigh of satisfaction, she caressed his calf with the sole of one foot, parting her legs to do so, making him aware of the soft skin of her inner thigh against his hip.

'Belle,' he breathed, and she ran caressing fingers over his scalp.

'Do you know, you're the first person who's ever called me that?' she whispered softly. 'I've been called Issy, and Ella on one occasion. But nobody's called me Belle before. Just you.'

'Belle...'

He didn't know why he said her name again. It was hardly a protest, even though his conscience was begging him not to repeat his mistake. It was just that she was so desirable, and so tempting, and a sly voice was reminding him that he should make it good for her too.

His hands moved, almost of their own volition, sliding down the warm curve of her body to cradle one half of her delicious rear. Then, as his teeth nipped the curve of her shoulder, he drew one finger between her legs, finding the moist heart of her womanhood, and the throbbing nub it protected.

With the heel of his hand stroking that responsive nub, he allowed his fingers to part the damp curls and find the source of her wetness. He could tell by her shallow breathing, and the way she jerked beneath his hands, that she had no real conception of what could happen. When he slid two fingers inside her, she fairly melted under his hands.

'Pat—rick,' she protested, her hands going automatically to stop him, and then halting some inches from their goal. 'Oh, God,' she whispered, and he knew it was happening for her. 'Oh, God, please—don't—don't stop,' she choked convulsively, and arched helplessly as the feelings took her beyond control.

She was still trembling when he took his hands away from her and slid down to kiss the damp skin between her breasts. Her hands clutched his head, pressing his face against her, and the ache between his thighs intensified again.

'Was it good?' he asked, knowing the answer but wanting to hear her say it for herself, and she swallowed convulsively before gazing down into his uptilted face.

'You know it was,' she said. 'But I thought—' She shook her head. 'Was that how it was for you?' She hesitated. 'I want to know.'

'It was better,' said Patrick huskily, sliding even lower and laving her navel with his tongue. 'Much better,' he added as the musky scent of her arousal rose up to him. He crushed his conscience. 'Do you want me to show you again?'

Isobel's brows drew together. 'Again?'

'Yes, again,' he agreed, knowing there was no way he was going to get out of this bed without having her once more. He spread her thighs with a lazy determination and moved between them. Then, nudging her moist core with his erection, he slid sinuously inside. 'God, that's good,' he said, the words wrung from him as her silky flesh enveloped him completely. 'So good,' he said again, and crushed her mouth beneath his lips.

He took it slowly this time, slow and easy, but even so it was hard when every nerve in his body wanted to explode with the incredible relief he knew was in the making. Still, he controlled himself and stayed with her, every inch of the way, watching the way she clung to him, trusting him not to let her down.

And he didn't—nor himself either—his release coming only seconds after the rippling shudders of her climax racked her body. Those convulsing muscles were too much for him, and he uttered a hoarse cry as he let go. For several mind-blowing seconds, he was beyond guilt, beyond consciousness, beyond anything but the conviction that this woman was his natural mate...

CHAPTER NINE

How had it happened?

Isobel dismissed the foolish question. She knew perfectly well how it had happened. What she couldn't understand was why, and she was sure the answer to that was going to be a lot harder to find.

She heaved a sigh.

So, what were the facts? She had let a man she scarcely knew—and who possibly made a habit of seducing gullible women—to make love to her, and she had only herself to blame if she was regretting it now.

Isobel's jaw compressed.

Was she regretting it? Was she regretting that, after twenty-eight years of celibacy, twenty-eight years of having no inclination to let any man that close to her, let alone to allow him to climb into her bed, she had lost her virginity to a man about whom she knew precisely nothing?

She wasn't absolutely sure.

The truth was, she was still dazed by what had happened. Her experience of men—such as it was—had never led her to believe that she might ever be in such a position. The stories she'd heard, the fiction she'd read had given her a faintly cynical view of sex and its connotations, and although several men had tried to change her mind their hot breath and searching hands had soon discouraged her.

Patrick Riker had changed all that.

From the moment he'd touched her, from the moment he'd laid his hands on her and kissed her with his hard, possessive mouth, she'd been totally out of her depth. Emotions she hadn't even known existed had taken possession of her and, far from backing off, she had given in to him, almost without a protest. Instead of keeping her head, she'd lost it—totally—and so much more besides.

She moistened her dry lips.

If it wasn't so incredible, it would be laughable, she thought ruefully. She could just imagine what Chris would say if she ever found out what she'd done. For years she'd been urging her employer to shed her inhibitions and get some fun out of life, but even she would have a problem with last night's scenario.

Dear God, she didn't even know how to get in touch with him. He'd left, as he'd arrived, without offering any excuse for doing so, and as far as she knew she might never see him again.

Oh, he'd said he'd be in touch. As he'd fastened his belt and stuffed his shirt into his waistband he'd promised he'd ring her, but she only had his word for that. She'd still been enveloped in the mellow afterglow of his lovemaking when he'd left, and she now conceded wryly that she'd have believed anything he said at that time. It was only now, a little more than eight hours later, that the less pleasant aspects of the situation were becoming apparent, and she was beginning to realise how reckless she had been.

She could be pregnant!

Her breath caught in her throat. He hadn't used any protection and, God knew, she had never needed any. Even now, her body could be incubating his seed, offering it sustenance, helping to form the baby that he had given her. Was she going to be just another single mother? Another statistic? One of those poor women who up till now, if she was honest, she had given little thought to?

'How are the mighty fallen . . . !' she thought glumly. It served her right for being so arrogant. What was that expression about chickens coming home to roost? She had certainly proved that there was no such word as never.

Getting up from the breakfast bar, she caught sight of the kitchen clock and groaned. She'd promised her mother that she'd take her to the hospital this morning, and now she was going to be late. But although she felt some relief that she was not expected to open the shop today she hadn't given a thought as to the reason why. And she simply wasn't in the mood to have an argument with her mother. Not when she was half afraid that Mrs Herriot might guess what had happened. Isobel felt sure the events of the night before were emblazoned on her face for all to see.

Coming to a decision, she picked up the portable phone and pulled out the aerial.

It rang at least a dozen times before her mother answered. 'Yes?'

'Mum?'

'Isobel?' Her mother sounded put out. 'Where are you?'

'At home.' Isobel hesitated. 'I'm sorry. I'm afraid I'm not going to be able to take you into Stratford this morning.'

'You're not?'

Her mother's tone was peevish now, and Isobel squashed the feelings of guilt that the words engendered. 'I—no,' she said firmly. 'I'm—not well.'

'Not well? You were perfectly all right yesterday evening. What's wrong? Do you want your father to come and have a look at you?'

'No!' Heaven forbid! 'No, I—I've just got a pretty bad headache, that's all. I—didn't sleep very well last night.' Liar!

'Really?' Mrs Herriot sounded even less sympathetic now. 'Couldn't you take a tablet?'

'I could—I *have*.' Isobel crossed her fingers. 'Only I'm not even dressed yet, and you have to be there for half past ten, don't you?'

'Heavens, yes.' Isobel could almost see her mother looking at her watch. 'Well, how am I supposed to manage? I can't drive.'

Isobel sighed. 'Couldn't Daddy take you?'

'Your father has surgery, as you very well know.'

'Does he?' Isobel had thought it was her father's turn for evening surgery. 'Well, a taxi, then.'

'Do you have any idea how much a taxi would cost?'

Isobel's shoulders sagged. 'All right. I'll pay.'

'I couldn't let you do that. And the money's not the point.' Isobel had thought it was. 'It's the inconvenience. What if I get a driver who smokes?'

'All right, I'll come.' Isobel couldn't stand any more of this. 'Give me twenty minutes.'

'Are you sure, dear?'

Isobel winced at the synthetic sympathy that accompanied those words. 'Yes, I'm sure,' she said, rather shortly, and rang off.

She was securing her hair in its usual plait when someone knocked at the door, and she sighed. Why was it that she always had visitors just as she was either getting dressed to go out or planning a quiet evening—?

Her breath caught in her throat.

Patrick! What if it was Patrick? It could be. He could have spent the night at a hotel in Horsham and come back. After the way she had been decrying his behaviour earlier, it would serve her right if it was him. What if he asked to see her again tonight? How was she going to respond?

Her pulses raced. There was only one way to find out. But she would have to be brief. Her mother had an appointment at the hospital, and she was already going to have to break the speed limit to get her there on time.

Richard Gregory stood on the threshold.

For a moment she was so disappointed that it was him that she couldn't say anything, and his fair features darkened with his usual flush of colour.

But then common courtesy forced her to acknowledge him, and, hardly aware that she was checking the buttons of her long chemise dress with a nervous hand, she said, 'What are you doing here?'

'I might ask you the same question,' countered Richard, with just a trace of resentment in his tone. 'Shouldn't you be at the shop? It is half past nine, you know.'

'Is it really?' Isobel drew a calming breath. 'And I've got to be in Stratford in less than an hour.' She refused to ask how he came to be there so early. 'What do you want, Richard? Whatever it is I'm afraid you're going to have to be quick.'

A flash of impatience crossed his face, but was swiftly banished. 'Perhaps I can be of service,' he said, without answering her question. 'It's obvious you're in something of a panic, and it's not wise to drive if you're worrying about the time. I'll take you to Stratford, and bring you back, if you like. That way you can relax until you get there.'

'No—'

'I insist.'

'You don't understand...' Isobel resented having to explain, but it seemed there was nothing else for it. 'I'm taking my mother to Stratford. She's got an appointment at the hospital. Now, if you don't mind, I'd like to finish getting ready. And I'm not opening the shop today.'

Richard's mouth turned down. 'Why not?'

'Because—' Isobel struggled to keep her temper '—because I have other commitments.' She wished he would go. She was no longer interested in why he'd come. Just in how soon she could get rid of him.

'So...' he paused to give his words significance '...you're not interested in what I've managed to find out about the leases.' He half turned away. 'I'm sorry. I had thought it was important to you.'

Isobel closed her eyes. 'Of course it's important to me!' she exclaimed, wishing he didn't make her feel so ungrateful. She opened her eyes again to find him watching her with calculated malice. 'It's just—well, I don't have the time to discuss it now. Couldn't you come to the shop— say, tomorrow?'

'I shan't be in Horsham tomorrow,' he replied curtly. And then, before she could think of an alternative arrangement, he said, 'I could come back this evening. Perhaps we could talk about it over dinner?'

Isobel's jaw clamped. 'I can't,' she said at once, almost automatically. The idea of having dinner with Richard Gregory didn't appeal at all.

'Oh, well...' His reaction was to lose any trace of amiability that still lingered. 'You'll hear about it soon enough, I dare say. My boss doesn't let the grass grow under his feet.'

Isobel wanted to scream. First her mother, now this. 'All right,' she said recklessly as he was about to open the gate

at the foot of the path, 'I'll be back about—say, one o'clock.
I could meet you for a drink if you like. How about the
bar of The Green Dragon at a quarter past?'

Richard looked doubtful. 'The Green Dragon? Where's
that?'

'Across the road from the shop,' said Isobel. 'And now
I really have to go. My mother will be having a fit!'

He accepted the arrangement, much to Isobel's relief,
and she shut the door again and finished getting ready. She
didn't know why, but she pushed the safety chain into position as she went upstairs. There was something about
Richard Gregory that she didn't altogether trust.

Of course, he didn't come back, and her precaution
proved unnecessary, but she still had that uneasy feeling
when she left the house. It was foolish, really, because he'd
done nothing to earn her suspicion.

Unlike Patrick... But that was another story.

Her temper wasn't improved when she arrived at Warwick
Road to find that her mother had already left for the
hospital.

'Liz Stuart turned up, so she offered to take her,' declared her father rather tersely, not very pleased to be pulled
out of surgery to give his daughter an explanation. 'Don't
blame me. You knew she had an appointment. You
shouldn't have been late.'

'No.'

Isobel had no answer to that, and as if suddenly remembering the excuse she had offered her mother Dr Herriot
gave her a studied look. 'Are you all right?'

Isobel's nails dug into her palms. 'Of course I'm all right.'
Her lips twitched. 'Why wouldn't I be?'

'Well, I thought you'd told your mother that the reason
you were late was because you were not well,' retorted her
father curtly. 'I must say, I didn't believe it myself, but,
looking at you now, I'm not so sure.'

'What do you mean?'

He frowned. 'I don't know. You look a little strained,
that's all. You're not worried about anything, are you? If
you're afraid you're losing custom at the shop looking after

your mother, then say the word. I'm sure she's quite capable of making a cup of tea when she wants one, and I can always ask Mrs Finch to do the shopping.'

Isobel sighed. 'I don't mind looking after her.'

'I didn't ask you if you minded,' returned her father, just as his nurse came into the hall. 'All right, Marie, I know I've got patients waiting.' He turned back to his daughter. 'Just give a little thought to what I've said.'

'I will.'

But as Isobel left him to go into her parents' living room it was not his words that brought the unwelcome heat to her face and neck. It was the knowledge that she was vulnerable. That she was incapable of keeping her feelings to herself.

CHAPTER TEN

'YOU didn't see her, did you?'

'As I said, the shop was closed,' said Patrick obliquely. 'Her—her mother's ill, or something. Her assistant came by as I was looking in the window. She told me about it.'

Jillian pursed her lips. 'So you didn't see her?'

Patrick weighed the alternatives. 'How could I?'

'You could have asked the assistant where she lived.'

'And done what?' Patrick was amazed at his own duplicity. 'What excuse did I have to ask where she lived? I hardly know the woman.'

'You've spoken to her, haven't you?'

'Well—yes.'

'So couldn't you have made up some reason why you wanted to get in touch with her? For pity's sake, Pat, the woman's poisoning my marriage. I'd have thought that warranted some effort on your behalf.'

Patrick said nothing. For one of the few times in his life, he felt himself at a loss for words. There was no way he could tell his sister that he'd slept with Isobel Herriot. The consequences of that didn't bear thinking about, even if he could offer the excuse that it had been a way of deflecting her attention from Richard.

Because whoever had spent the night at The Coach House with his brother-in-law it hadn't been Isobel. Indeed, he wondered now if Isobel had been lying about their relationship. Had she really gone out with Richard, as she'd implied, or had that been a defence mechanism? And if they were *friends*—a situation he found no more palatable than before, but for different reasons—how long would it be before his brother-in-law attempted to—to—?

To do what he had already done? he finished bleakly. To take advantage of a woman who was totally unaware of her own sensuality? His palms felt unpleasantly damp suddenly, and he thrust them into his jacket pockets. Dammit, it was he who should be berating his sister, not the other way about. She'd got him into this—with no good reason, as it had turned out.

'So what did you do?' Jillian demanded now, and for a moment Patrick's stare was uncomprehending. 'Last night,' his sister prompted, annoyed by his apparent abstraction. 'For goodness' sake, Pat, what's the matter with you? Haven't you woken up yet? It's the middle of the afternoon!'

That was the trouble, thought Patrick grimly. He'd slept too heavily, and for too long. A case of enforced oblivion. But he couldn't tell her that, could he?

'I'm awake,' he replied shortly, and Jillian sneered.

'You surprise me.'

'What do you mean?'

'Well, you didn't exactly waste the evening, did you?' she countered. 'I spoke to Mum this morning. She phoned while you were still in bed. She said you didn't arrive until after midnight. Despite the fact that you were supposed to be having supper with her.'

Patrick's jaw compressed. 'I got held up.'

'I'll bet you did.'

'What's that supposed to mean?'

'Who held you up? Isobel Herriot's assistant?'

'No!' Patrick glared at her.

'Who, then? Joe?'

'Joe?' Patrick frowned. 'He wasn't with me.'

'Wasn't he?' His sister didn't sound as if she believed him. 'Well, you and he have been known to—what's the expression?—*tie one on*, from time to time.'

'As I say, Joe wasn't with me.'

'But you don't deny it was late when you got to Kerrymore?'

Patrick scowled. Very late, he reflected silently. And not just because it had been after eleven when he'd left Isobel's. He'd spent a good hour or more sitting in the car in a secluded lay-by, wondering if he could invent an excuse not to visit his mother at all.

'I don't have to confirm or deny anything,' he said now. 'And as you don't appear to trust me I don't think there's any point in continuing this discussion.'

'Oh, there is.' Jillian seemed to realise she had gone too far. 'Pat, please—'

But before she could finish what she had been about to say a door slammed, and Jillian turned a frowning face towards the window. 'Who—?'

It was Richard.

Before Patrick could move, his brother-in-law appeared in the open doorway. He didn't know who was the most surprised, Richard or himself, but there was no denying the look of dismay that crossed his brother-in-law's face when he saw who was there.

'Pat!' he exclaimed blankly. 'I didn't know you were coming down.'

'Obviously,' said Patrick tersely, thanking his lucky stars that Richard hadn't chosen to disregard his orders twenty-four hours sooner. 'Aren't you supposed to be in Amsterdam?'

Richard gave them both a resentful look. 'I—missed the flight.'

'Then why didn't you take the next?' asked Patrick tautly. 'As I recall, there were several alternatives.'

'I wasn't well,' declared Richard at once, and for all her professed distrust of her husband Jillian looked immediately concerned.

'Oh, Rich!' she exclaimed, crossing the room to take hold of his arm with anxious fingers. 'What is it, darling? What's the matter? You do look pale now I come to think of it.'

Patrick's hands balled into fists in his pockets. God, he thought, was Jillian totally green? There'd been nothing wrong with Richard—not until he'd seen his brother-in-law standing in his living room. Then, like Patrick, he'd seized on the first excuse that came to mind. Only in his case he'd been trying to protect his sister, Patrick defended himself firmly. He didn't yet know what Richard's agenda was.

'It's nothing,' declared the other man now, allowing Jillian to help him into a comfortable armchair. 'I spent the night at the airport, and then drove home this morning. I did intend to phone you, but—'

'Never mind that now.' Jillian was never happier than when she was fussing over him. 'Look, Pat was just leaving, weren't you?' Her eyes passed an appealing message to her brother. 'You can get someone else to go to Amsterdam, can't you?'

As Richard's trip had been a deliberate ploy to get him out of the way, there was really no argument.

'I—sure,' said Patrick drily. 'Sure, why not? I might even go myself. Those apartments we're renovating on the Amstelpark are behind schedule.'

'Oh, good.' Jillian assured her husband that she wouldn't be a moment, and then escorted her brother to the door. 'Um—thanks for trying,' she said, in a hushed voice. 'I'll talk to you again later. I suppose you're going back to London now?'

Patrick hesitated. 'Jill—'

'We can't talk now,' she declared swiftly, with an apprehensive glance over her shoulder. 'Poor Rich; he does look under the weather, doesn't he? You won't expect him back at work before next week, will you?'

Patrick's expression hardened. 'I'll expect him back at work on Friday, as in tomorrow,' he replied. 'I'm sure you'll see he makes it. We wouldn't want him to lose touch with his responsibilities.'

Jillian looked mutinous, but she didn't argue. 'If he's well enough, he'll be there,' was the best she would offer. 'Thank you for calling, Patrick. I'm sorry it was such a—wasted journey.'

Patrick got back into the Porsche, and drove out of the gates to his sister's house in a foul mood. It wasn't just the knowledge that Richard had lied to him or that Jillian had reacted so predictably to his brother-in-law's pathetic schemes that was bugging him. The truth was, he didn't like what he had done, and he resented that. He wasn't in the habit of seducing women, unless they initiated it, and the knowledge that he'd been misled left a bitter taste in his mouth.

He thought about going back to the cottage to see Isobel, but despite the sharp stab of desire that that evoked he tamped the feeling down. There was nothing to be gained by going back to Horsham, not unless he had some intention of continuing their relationship. And that particular idea simply wasn't feasible. She'd never believe that his intentions were innocent, not when she found out who he really was.

Besides, he reminded himself, he wasn't interested in starting another relationship. Despite their occasional spats, he and Joanna got along very well together. She suited him. She was neither carelessly indifferent nor overly possessive. And there had never been any question of who was controlling the affair.

Isobel was different. He didn't like it, but even after just one night he knew she could be dangerous to his peace of mind. With her he wasn't in control; if that had been so, he would never have lost his head. Besides which she was the type of woman who would expect a total commitment, and that definitely was not what he wanted.

So, despite an almost painful urge to ignore this reasoning, Patrick did the sensible thing and drove back to London. But it had been a singularly disastrous twenty-four hours, he thought grimly as he parked the sports car in front of his house. He'd made love to a woman who was supposed to be his brother-in-law's mistress and wasn't; he'd let his mother down, first by not arriving in time to have supper with her and then by sleeping so long that the only conversation she'd had with him was over lunch; and, to cap it all, Richard hadn't gone to Holland. He'd turned up, like the bad penny he undoubtedly was, almost catching Patrick in the act.

God, the idea that his brother-in-law might have driven straight to Horsham to see Isobel brought him out in a cold sweat. Not only would Richard have found a malicious delight in telling Isobel exactly who he was, but he could imagine Jillian's horror when he carried the news to her. The fact that Richard would have had to explain exactly what he was doing in Horsham would have been a small price to pay for his brother-in-law's humiliation. Besides, he had just proved he could wrap Jillian round his little finger. Patrick didn't believe a word of his excuses for not going to Amsterdam.

It was bloody ludicrous, he thought, getting out of the car and slamming the door with unnecessary force. It was a farce. Not five minutes before Richard had shown up Jillian had been berating him for not exposing her husband's infidelity. Then Richard had appeared, pretended he was sick, and Jillian had been all over him. She'd swallowed his story completely, like the gullible fool she always was.

Well, he'd had enough, decided Patrick savagely. If his sister still believed Richard was having an affair with Isobel, then she would have to find someone else to deal with it. He was sick of all the lies, sick of half-truths and prevarications. From now on he was going to be too busy to spend time acting as Jillian's unpaid sleuth.

The fact that he was responsible for some of those half-truths and prevarications was not something he chose to dwell on in the days ahead. It helped to do what he had told his sister and brother-in-law he intended to do and leave the country. Several days in Amsterdam did help him to get the situation into perspective, and by the time he came back to England he had almost succeeded in convincing himself that what had happened had not been his fault.

The urge to see Isobel again was still there, of course, but he suppressed it. He couldn't afford to risk his credibility by exposing his infatuation. He regretted having to let her down, but he assured himself that she would soon get over it. It wasn't as if there was any emotional attachment. And sooner or later some man would have taken her virginity. It was unfortunate it had had to be him in one way, yet in another it was better for her. At least he hadn't hurt her. Well—no more than he'd had to, he amended, and afterwards he'd made it good for her too.

* * *

His equilibrium was shattered on his first night back in England.

He phoned Joanna from the airport and invited her to have dinner with him that evening, and she was delighted to accept.

'I thought you must have found someone else,' she confessed, revealing her own uncertainties, and Patrick was quick to reassure her that it had just been pressure of work that had dictated his movements.

'We'll eat at the club,' he said, knowing how much she liked to visit the exclusive hostelry in St James's. 'I'll pick you up at about half past seven, OK?'

'OK,' she agreed, at once, obviously eager to see him. 'I've missed you, Pat. Don't be late.'

'I won't.'

He hung up the phone, collected his luggage from the carousel, and went in search of Joe. Already he felt more optimistic. He was getting his life back on track, and it felt good.

That was why it was such a devastating blow when the comfortable cocoon he had fashioned for himself was shattered.

He arrived at Joanna's apartment with at least half an hour to spare before they needed to leave for the restaurant. He had a gift for her—a delicate spray of diamonds and emeralds that he'd bought for her in Amsterdam—and he had every intention of renewing their physical relationship before they left for the club.

The fact that he didn't actually take up her offer of intimacy was due entirely to the unwelcome memories of Isobel that still lingered. When Joanna opened the door to him, clad only in a black satin teddy, he was unhappily reminded of Isobel's tall, lissom body. Joanna's perhaps more fashionable stature was superimposed by Isobel's more generous frame, and although he was not unduly worried by the comparison it certainly cooled any ardour he might have been feeling.

Still, Joanna was suitably thrilled with the expensive brooch, and any momentary awkwardness quickly fled. Instead of tumbling her onto her bed, Patrick contented himself with a glass of the single malt she kept especially for his enjoyment, and by the time she reappeared, slim and elegant in a black, ankle-length sheath, he had convinced himself that the evening was safely back on course.

Joe was waiting with the car, and he soon whisked them to their destination. As Patrick had every intention of spending the night with Joanna, he dismissed Joe, assuring him that they'd take a cab back to the apartment when the meal was over.

Patrick was well-known at the establishment, and after drinks and hors d'oeuvres in the members' bar they were shown to a secluded table for two. The restaurant was large, and well patronised, but discreet arrangements of tropical foliage gave ample room for privacy, while a string quartet playing in the background prevented confidential conversations from being overheard.

'This is so nice,' enthused Joanna, reaching across the table to squeeze his hand, and because he felt he had been rather churlish earlier Patrick turned his fingers so that he could return the pressure.

And that was when he saw her.

She and Richard were sitting just a short distance away, and his whole body froze in sudden distaste. Though that wasn't the word to use; it didn't encompass half the repugnance he was feeling. As he continued to stare at her, he felt as if he was in the throes of some traumatic shock.

God!

'Pat!'

Joanna made a sound of protest, and for a moment he thought he had said the word out loud. But then he realised that she was trying to release her fingers. In his horrified state, he was mangling her hand, and the little laugh she uttered was only partly humorous.

'Darling!' she exclaimed. 'You're almost breaking my wrist!' And as he forced his fingers to relax Isobel looked up from her plate and saw him too.

CHAPTER ELEVEN

IT WAS him!

Isobel could hardly believe it, but it was true. Of all the places for Richard to choose, it was incredible that he should have brought her into Patrick Riker's orbit. He was the last man on earth she wanted to see, and, judging by his expression, she was the last woman he wanted to see as well.

It hurt.

Despite having had more than two weeks to come to terms with the fact that she was never going to see Patrick Riker again, she was still hurt. How could he do a thing like that? she wondered. How could he take advantage of her and disappear without a second's concern? For all he knew she could be pregnant. He'd known she was a virgin, after all.

She drew a trembling breath. He wasn't alone. Which was probably why she hadn't seen him again, she acknowledged, trying to be pragmatic. She'd known from the moment she saw him that a man like Patrick Riker would never be short of female companionship. What she hadn't expected was that she would be just another victim of his ego.

It angered her. It angered her more that just looking at him made her feel weak. Dammit, the man was a bastard, and she'd been right to compare him to Charles Ankrum. Only her erstwhile boss had never stood a chance of seducing her, whereas Patrick Riker had found it all too easy.

Her hand tightened around the stem of her fork, the knuckles showing white through her pale skin. She wished she could take the fork and stab him with it. He deserved to suffer some retribution for what he'd done.

She wondered who the woman was. She supposed she could be his wife, but somehow she doubted it. Wives didn't usually gaze at their husbands with quite that degree of intimacy—not in her experience, anyway—and, although she had no reason to trust him, he had said he was no longer married.

No, he wouldn't be, she decided bitterly. Marriage entailed too much of a commitment, and a man like him would always want his freedom. Even Richard, pathetic as he was, admitted having made the mistake of tying himself to the wrong woman. Ordinary men made mistakes and paid for them. Men like Patrick Riker never did.

'Is something wrong?'

Richard had suddenly noticed that she wasn't listening to him. It had taken him a full minute to realise that Isobel's attention had moved elsewhere. But then, even Richard secretly considered he was irresistible. Why else had she agreed to have dinner with him? After all, he'd told her he'd succeeded in fixing the rents at a reasonable rate.

Isobel wasn't sure now why she had decided to have dinner with him. She could have spent the night alone, having room service at the hotel. But when she'd agreed to chauffeur her mother to London, because Mrs Herriot wanted to attend an evening seminar on interior design and technology, it had seemed like a good idea. At least it had silenced her mother's continual demands for her to socialise, and there had seemed no danger of meeting anyone she knew at Richard's club.

It was the first time she had spent an evening with him, though she doubted Patrick Riker would believe her. In his world, men and women slept together inconsequentially. It was only women like her who broke the mould.

Richard was getting impatient. He didn't like being ignored. It was obvious that Isobel's thoughts were focused on something—or someone—beyond their table, and the knowledge infuriated him. He hadn't brought her out for the evening so that she could spend her time making eyes at other men, and he swung round in his chair, prepared to give any would-be Romeo a hard look.

He turned back almost immediately, his cheeks flaming and a look of consternation on his face. 'Pat,' he muttered,

scarcely aware that the word was audible, but Isobel had
heard him, and now her attention was fixed firmly on him.

'What did you say?' she asked, staring at him, and
Richard made an involuntary gesture.

'When?'

'Just now,' said Isobel tautly, uncaring that he looked
dismayed. 'You said *Pat,* didn't you?' She licked her lips.
'Do you know that man?'

'What man?'

Richard was being deliberately obtuse and Isobel's mood
went from raw humiliation to angry resolution. 'That man,'
she said, nodding towards Patrick's table. 'I distinctly heard
you say "Pat". Now are you going to deny it, or shall I
invite him over here to clear this up?'

'*No!*' Richard's denial was urgent. 'For God's sake don't
invite him over here.' His brows drew together. 'Are you
saying you know him?' He gave an impatient shrug. 'You
never said.'

Isobel thought of denying it, but she intended to get to
the bottom of this, so there didn't seem much point. 'Why
should I?' she asked. 'What's he to you?'

'You should know,' retorted Richard shortly, 'considering he's my boss. And my brother-in-law, as well. I
suppose he told you that too?'

Isobel's jaw sagged. 'You mean that's Mr *Shannon?*'

'I thought you said you knew him.'

Isobel swallowed. 'I've—met him,' she admitted cau-
tiously. 'And your wife is his sister? Is that what you're
saying?'

'Unfortunately, yes.' Richard slumped in his seat. 'Oh,
God, why did I think of coming here?'

'You said it was your club,' Isobel reminded him evenly,
aware that her brain was managing to function on two levels
at once. On one she could talk to Richard almost casually,
as if what he had just told her had not dealt her a shattering
blow. But on the other she was frantically trying to deal
with the implications, with the knowledge that Patrick
Shannon had been lying to her all along.

'Well, it's not,' muttered Richard now, evidently deciding there was no point in pretending otherwise. 'I used Pat's name to get in. I've done it before. It's no skin off his nose.'

'Except on this occasion,' murmured Isobel, putting down her fork. Her heart almost stopped beating as she saw Patrick get up from his seat. 'I think he's coming over.'

The way Richard thrust back his chair and got to his feet, Isobel might have been forgiven for thinking he was about to run for it. But instead of that Richard went to meet Patrick. He evidently hoped to mask their exchange with the steady hum of noise.

But in this case he was disappointed. Ignoring his brother-in-law's attempts to detain him, Patrick continued on towards their table, his eyes narrowing grimly as he took in Isobel's cold expression.

'Hello again,' he said, and Isobel wondered if he was aware of how much she longed to scratch his eyes out at that moment. As he stood there, tall and self-confident, in his charcoal-grey suit, which had evidently been designed with his lean frame in mind, and with a look of cool indifference on his face, she had never hated anyone so much. 'This is an unexpected pleasure.'

'Is it?' Uncaring what Richard, who was hovering at the other man's elbow, might think, Isobel refused to let Patrick see how devastated she really was. 'I understand I have you to thank for the minimal increase in our rents. It was kind of you to consider us, when you would obviously have preferred to move us out.'

Patrick's mouth tightened. 'I don't think there was ever any question of the tenants being asked to move out, was there?' he countered, evidently not prepared to let her have it all her own way. 'If I gave you that impression, I'm sorry. It's sometimes easy to misinterpret events.'

'Isn't it?' Isobel was amazed at the way her lips curled into a sardonic smile, almost without her volition. 'Oh, well, please don't let us keep you. I'm sure your—wife?—must be wondering what's going on.'

'I told you, I don't have a wife,' retorted Patrick harshly, and then cast a warning look at Richard's wide-eyed face. 'But perhaps you're right—this isn't the time to conduct this conversation.' He sucked in a breath. 'I'll see you tomorrow, Richard. Goodnight, Miss Herriot.'

He strode away, and although she was sure that Richard would have preferred to make his getaway he dropped back into his chair. Isobel herself was trembling—so badly, in fact, that she was very much afraid that she couldn't have left her seat at that moment even if her life had depended on it. Fencing with Patrick might be intellectually satisfying, but it was also physically draining.

'Supercilious bastard!' muttered Richard, pushing his plate aside and taking an enormous gulp of his wine. Then, ignoring the approaching waiter, he refilled his glass himself, waving the man away with an impatient hand.

Isobel moistened her lips. 'Do you want to go?'

Richard snorted. 'What do you think?' he said, swallowing another mouthful of wine. 'God, I thought he was still in Amsterdam. He must have got home earlier today.'

Isobel clasped her hands together in her lap. 'He's been in Amsterdam?'

'Haven't I just said so?' Richard seemed to consider the fact that he'd been exposed removed any need for him to be civil. 'I was supposed to go to Holland but I got out of it.' He grunted. 'Which will be something else to beat me with tomorrow.'

'To beat you with?' Isobel frowned. 'I'm afraid I—'

'I'm married to his sister!' exclaimed Richard irritably. 'Don't you understand? I bet he can't wait to tell Jill all about it.' He groaned. 'I don't think I'll bother going home tonight.'

Isobel blinked. 'But you said—'

'What? What did I say?'

'That—that you and your wife were having problems. I understood that you were practically separated; that your wife didn't care what you did.'

Richard gave her a dour look. 'So what? Part of it's true, anyway. We are having problems. Due in no small part to *his* interference, if you must know.'

Isobel gasped. 'So you lied to me!'

Richard scowled. 'Doesn't everybody?' He viewed her pale face without remorse. 'Don't look at me as if I'm the only one who's been keeping secrets. How come you know Pat? That's what I want to know.'

She took a breath. 'In the circumstances, I don't think that's any of your business.'

'Don't you, by God?' Richard stared at her angrily. 'Well, I bloody do, as it happens. Has that sod been poking around behind my back?'

Isobel suspected that that was exactly what Patrick had been doing, but she had no intention of admitting that to Richard. Nor did it excuse the way Patrick had treated her. She despised the pair of them, and she wished there were some way she could get even.

'I think I'd like to go,' she said, without answering him, and Richard regarded her with a sullen, vengeful look.

'I'm not stopping you,' he said, clearly deciding he had nothing to gain by taking her back to her hotel. 'See you around, as they say. I doubt if I'll be visiting Horsham in the near future.'

It would be all the same if you were, thought Isobel malevolently, relieved to find that she had regained the use of her legs. Without looking in Patrick's direction again, she left the restaurant, hoping there would be a taxi waiting outside.

'Isobel!'

Patrick's voice arrested her just as the commissionaire was opening the door for her. She would have ignored him had she been alone, but with the doorman looking on it would have appeared churlish not to acknowledge the summons. But her lips were pressed tightly together as he strode towards her, and she refused to meet the eyes that raked her face.

'Where are you going?'

Once again, Isobel's eyes were drawn to the doorman, and as if sensing that he was in the way the man hastily withdrew into his small kiosk. But he was still watching them, and Isobel found she couldn't say nothing, even if her instincts were telling her to do exactly that.

So, in a controlled voice, she said crisply, 'Where do you think?'

Patrick was displeased. She still refused to look at him, but she could sense his displeasure in the unevenness of his breathing and the sudden stiffening of his body. 'Richard isn't escorting you?' he asked. 'He's not taking you back to your—what?—hotel?' He expelled a breath, and the heat of it moved the hair on her temples. 'Dammit, he can't just abandon you like this! I'll go and get him—'

'Don't you dare!' Isobel looked up then, the anger his words had inspired giving her the courage to face him down. 'Just get out of my way, Patrick. I don't need anyone's help, least of all yours.'

He swore then, softly but very distinctly, his anger communicating itself to her through the savage tone of his voice. 'You don't understand,' he continued harshly. 'Tell me where you're staying. I think we need to talk.'

'You wish!' The look she gave him mingled scorn and incredulity in equal measures. 'No, Patrick. You had plenty of time to talk at the cottage. Now, do you mind? I think I can see a taxi waiting.'

'Belle—'

'Don't call me that!'

'Why not?' His dark brows arched almost insultingly. 'You didn't object before.'

'Which shows what a fool I was,' she replied, reaching for the doorhandle. 'Enjoy your evening, Patrick. I'm sure your ladyfriend will be far more eager than I was.'

His face hardened. 'It takes two, Isobel.'

'Does it?' She refused to give him the satisfaction of thinking she had welcomed his attentions. 'I trusted you, Patrick, and you took advantage of me. You knew I'd never done anything like that before.'

He had the grace to look slightly ashamed then, his dark features showing a trace of colour. 'I know,' he conceded, his tone softer now. 'I'm not denying it. If it's any consolation, I've never done anything like that before either.'

'You liar!'

She stared at him, aghast, and as if suddenly aware that this was hardly the place to be having such a conversation Patrick interposed his bulk between her and the doorman's kiosk. 'I meant—I didn't know you had never—well, you know what I mean.'

'Do I?'

'Hell, yes. It was a new experience for me too.'

Isobel stared at him coldly. 'Is that supposed to be an apology?'

'Do you want an apology?' His eyes darkened dangerously. 'Don't you think you're making too much of this? It happened. It possibly shouldn't have, but it did. There's nothing I can do about it now.'

'Isn't there?' Isobel's eyes glittered, but only she knew it was the tears she was valiantly trying to suppress that gave them that unnatural sparkle. 'I suppose your sister put you up to it,' she added, wanting to die when she saw the sudden shocked awareness that crossed his face. 'What's the matter? Was she afraid Richard and I were getting too friendly?'

Patrick's features stiffened. 'It's not inconceivable.'

'But you and I know it's not true, don't we?'

'Do we?' The accusation in his voice lanced through her, and she was again assailed with the desire to make him suffer as she was suffering.

'You know we do!' she exclaimed as her mind darted here and there, trying to think of a similarly crippling rejoinder. 'Believe it or not, this is the first time I've ever spent an evening with him.'

'You said your relationship was serious,' he said coolly, reminding her of the foolish defence she'd put up against his advances. He frowned. 'What were you saying about me lying?'

Isobel caught her breath. 'You're totally without conscience, aren't you?'

'No.' He sighed. 'I'm pragmatic, that's all. I'm sorry if my interpretation of events doesn't agree with yours, but that's probably because I'm not letting emotion cloud the issue—'

'You bastard!'

Isobel stared at him with hate-filled eyes, frustration at her helplessness causing her hands to clench and every nerve in her body to tighten in thwarted fury.

'Belle—'

'Don't say that!'

'All right, Isobel, then. What is this all about? Can't you see—?'

'I'm pregnant!'

The words slipped from her tongue with such conviction that Isobel wondered how long she had been nurturing such an outrageous lie. And for all the shame she felt at perpetrating such a wicked deception it was almost worth it to see the undisguised horror in his face.

CHAPTER TWELVE

'YOU'RE lying!'

Patrick jerked upright in bed, sweat gushing from every pore in his body. God, had he said the words out loud? He could just imagine Mrs Joyce's reaction to that. He had always made a point of conducting his affairs far away from the almost chaste privacy of his own home, and he was not in the habit of talking in his sleep.

Aware that he was shaking, he sank back weakly against his pillows. He must have been having some crazy dream, he thought unsteadily. Thank God he was at home and not at Joanna's apartment. He wished he could remember what—

Isobel!

Her name ripped through his returning consciousness with much the same devastating effect that her words had had the night before. Dear God, he groaned silently, why would she do a thing like that? The words he had used then, and the words that had torn him from a peaceful slumber, were one and the same. He hadn't believed her then, and he didn't believe her now, but that didn't alter the fact that she had threatened the very foundations of the life he had made for himself.

He turned his head and looked at the clock on the bedside cabinet. It was a little after four—not late enough for it to be light but not early enough for him to try and get back to sleep. Even if he could, he acknowledged dourly. Dammit, she'd really screwed up his evening, and if he had disappointed Joanna earlier on, that was nothing compared to the way she had reacted when he'd got back to their table.

He closed his eyes against the images that assaulted his senses. But it was no good. He could still see Isobel's face when he'd accused her of lying, and the anguish in her expression had almost been his undoing.

But—and it was probably a good thing—when he'd reached for her she'd evaded him, charging out of the club and into the waiting cab without allowing him to say anything else. He hadn't even known where she was staying, and there was no way he could go back into the restaurant and demand that Richard give him the information.

Besides, the very idea of going back into the restaurant at that moment had been anathema to him. He had been in no state to face anyone, least of all his erstwhile mistress, and it had been at least another half-hour before, duly fortified with a handful of gulped malt whiskies, he'd returned to their table.

By then Joanna had been beyond pacification. Which was probably just as well, he conceded now. Anything that might have passed between them would have been purely functional, though he doubted now whether he could have functioned at all, in any capacity. Isobel had totally emasculated him, and he knew he would find it very hard to forgive her for doing that.

If he ever saw her again.

The thought of not doing so was somehow alien to him. Although he resented the way she had behaved, the idea that he might never see her again was not one he chose to embrace. Of course, he had to see her again, he told himself. He had to reassure himself that she had been lying, and discover what she considered he could have done to prevent what had happened.

He should have taken precautions, he reminded himself harshly. He should have given her no excuse to make such an accusation, true or otherwise. He'd never had a problem before. But then, he acknowledged reluctantly, he'd never wanted a woman as urgently, or as completely, as he'd wanted Isobel. He might be able to view his behaviour now with a certain amount of objectivity but that had certainly not been the case then. And, if he let himself remember, he could still feel the slick heat of her muscles holding him—

Swearing at the callowness of his reaction to these memories, Patrick thrust his legs out of the bed. A shower was what he needed, he decided. A cold shower, and then a couple of hours studying the plans for the marina development on Mykos. A leisure complex was a new departure for Shannon Holdings, and it might be exactly the kind of project he could make Richard responsible for.

Richard.

He scowled as he strode into the bathroom. He still hadn't decided what he was going to do about Richard. Sending him out of the country was one solution, or he could tell Jillian of his continuing association with Isobel and let her decide what she wanted to do. He'd pulled Richard off the Foxworth contract, but apparently that hadn't solved the problem.

The trouble was, it irked him to connect Richard's name with Isobel's. He suspected she hadn't been lying when she'd told him she hadn't been out with Richard before—or was that just wishful thinking?

In any case, he decided to play it by ear and let Richard make the running. The fact that his brother-in-law had left before he'd returned to the restaurant the night before was the only flaw in his analysis. But he refused to believe that Isobel would have welcomed Richard's reappearance when he had apparently been less than honest about his relationship with his wife. Patrick hadn't missed the rather heated exchange that had ensued after his intervention, and Isobel had been leaving when he'd caught up with her, after all.

He sighed. God, how uneventful his life had been up until a few weeks ago. In retrospect, even the threat Conrad Martin had represented seemed almost insignificant in comparison.

Which did not solve the problem of what to do about Isobel, he acknowledged later that morning as he chaired a meeting at the company offices in Portland Street. And he also knew that until he'd spoken to her again and cleared up the matter of the supposed pregnancy he wouldn't be able to concentrate on anything else. He'd already had to ask his finance director to repeat what he had said, twice, and it was obvious from the knowing glances of his colleagues that they assumed he was suffering the after-effects of a heavy date.

Well, he was, he reflected, with some irony. But this time an aspirin wouldn't cure it.

The shop was open.

Patrick had had Joe cruise along the high street past Caprice, and now he instructed the chauffeur to park in the car park behind The Green Dragon and get himself a drink while he conducted his business.

'You sure this is just going to be a flying visit?' asked Joe wryly, viewing his employer's grim features with some suspicion, and Patrick gave him a lacerating look.

'I've said so, haven't I?' he countered. 'This is just a—courtesy call, that's all. I have no desire to prolong it any longer than is absolutely necessary.'

'OK.'

Joe shrugged, and turned the big car into the yard of the pub that was across the road from the shop. He found a parking space that offered some protection from the strengthening rays of the sun, and then met Patrick's eyes in the rear-view mirror.

'Thank you.' Patrick thrust open his door and got out. 'I'll come and find you in—approximately fifteen minutes, right?'

'Right.'

Joe was unfailingly polite, and Patrick's expression dissolved into an unwilling grimace. 'OK, OK,' he said. 'I'm not in the best of tempers.' He slammed the door. 'It's nothing personal.'

Joe arched his dark brows in silent acknowledgement and, after delivering a frustrated slap to the body of the car, Patrick strode away.

Despite the fact that he had had to wait forty-eight hours before he could free himself to make this visit, now that he was here, Patrick felt a certain reluctance to complete his mission. Indeed, on the journey to Horsham he had half hoped Isobel might still be in London, thus aborting his attempt to speak to her today.

The trouble was, in the time that had elapsed between her outrageous announcement and his present situation the possibility that she might have been telling the truth had gained some credibility. It was all very well to dismiss her statement as the result of a belated desire to exact some revenge, but what if it was true? What if the reason why she had been so—so emotional was her condition?

Perhaps seeing him with Joanna—however innocent that encounter had been—had tipped her over the brink. Just because she had said nothing in front of Richard, that was no reason to assume that she'd only just thought of it. God, he was grateful she hadn't told Richard. He could just imagine the profit his brother-in-law would have made from that.

All the same, he now found himself curiously unwilling to pursue the matter. What if she was pregnant? What if even now she was nurturing the seed of his son or daughter inside her? How would he feel if he denied all knowledge of it, and then at some future date he saw her with the baby?

Of course, as he was seldom in this area, it was unlikely that he would ever accidentally see her with the child, but he knew himself well enough to know that whatever happened he would make a point of finding out, one way or the other. It was in his nature to see any situation through to its eventual conclusion, and no matter how he might feel now he would not be able to resist knowing the outcome.

He expelled a frustrated breath and glanced back at Joe, who had now emerged from the car and propped his bulky frame against the bonnet. It was annoying to think that Joe might know him better than he knew himself, and, suppressing any further introspection, he waited for a break in the traffic and crossed the road.

For once, Isobel was alone in the shop. She appeared to be dusting the shelves behind the counter, and he was able to enter the shop without warning her of his arrival.

'Can I help—?' she was beginning, turning to greet what she had evidently expected was another customer, but her lips clamped shut on the words when she saw him. With an obvious effort, she thrust the duster under the counter, and then gave him an icy look. 'What do you want?'

Patrick hesitated. Seeing her again had disturbed him, and he was irritably aware that for all his avowed intention of ending their association here and now he was still far too aware of her. She was wearing the spaghetti-strapped pinafore dress that she had worn that time they had gone to The Coach House, although this time she had a skinny-rib sweater on underneath, and although no one could have called her clothes fashionable she wore them with undeniable elegance.

Her hair was back in its braid, and although the last thing he wanted to do was relive the hours he had spent at the cottage he found himself wishing he could do as he had done then and release it from its severe confinement. She had looked so beautiful, with her hair a gold-streaked halo around her head as it rested on the pillow...

'I asked what you wanted,' she reminded him coldly. 'If you're looking for Richard, I haven't seen him again.'

Patrick took a step forward. 'I'm not looking for Richard,' he said evenly. 'As I said the other night, I think we need to talk.'

'Why?'

'Why?' Patrick gave her an impatient look. 'Come on, Isobel, you can't tell someone they're going to be a father and then expect them to forget about it.'

'Why not?' Isobel's expression didn't change. 'You find it easy to forget things.'

Patrick's jaw tightened. 'What things?'

She shrugged. 'Oh, little things—like your name's not Patrick Riker, it's Patrick *Shannon*. And the fact that Richard Gregory just happens to be your brother-in-law—which can hardly be a coincidence, can it?'

'I never said it was.'

'You never *said* anything,' retorted Isobel heatedly. 'You let me do all the talking, and, fool that I was, I thought it was because you were interested in me, not because you were checking up on your brother-in-law's movements.'

'It wasn't like that.' Patrick sighed, but she wouldn't listen to him.

'It was exactly like that,' she told him angrily. 'And just to make it a little more entertaining you decided to give his girlfriend a thrill by taking her to *your* bed. Only it wasn't *your* bed, it was *mine*, and I'll never forgive you for that.'

'For God's sake—'

'What?' She stared at him with cold, assessing eyes. 'Isn't this the usual reaction you get when you confer your attentions on someone? Well, I'm sorry. I'm afraid I don't know the proper way to respond to such a dubious honour, so you'd better go back to someone who does. That poor fool you were having dinner with, perhaps.'

Patrick breathed in deeply. She would not do this, he told himself grimly. She would not get him angry. She was hurt, and defiant, and perhaps she had some justification for feeling that way, but he was damned if he was going to give her the satisfaction of arousing him.

Yet that was exactly what she was doing, he realised furiously. With her pale face displaying a hectic colour, her soft lips parted, and the light of battle in her honey-brown eyes, she was magnificent, and his eyes were unwillingly drawn to the taut swell of her breasts. The nipples were button-hard and prominent, clearly outlined beneath the thin cotton garments she was wearing. The trouble was, he could remember them exactly like that, pressing against the skin of his torso, and it was impossible to ignore the undeniable effect she had on him.

'Belle,' he began steadily, and went on determinedly, ignoring her immediate demand that he should not call her that, 'Can't we at least be civil with one another? All right, perhaps I have been less than honest with you in the past, but my being here now has nothing to do with Richard or my sister and everything to do with you and me.'

'You and me?' She gazed at him as if he'd somehow taken leave of his senses. 'There is no "you and me". I—I'd like you to leave.'

Patrick swore. 'Belle, this is ridiculous! You can't announce that you're pregnant one day, and then pretend it hasn't happened the next.'

She held up her head. 'I'm not.'

'You're not what?' Patrick knew a moment's consternation.

'Pregnant,' she declared, gripping the counter with both hands. 'I made it up. Just as you thought.'

Patrick stared at her, aware that whatever his feelings had been when he'd come into the shop this was *not* what he wanted to hear now.

He shook his head. 'You're lying!'

Isobel's laugh had little mirth in it. 'You've said that before,' she said scornfully. 'Well, it really doesn't matter what you believe. It never did.' She squared her shoulders. 'Please go.'

Patrick's mouth compressed. 'This is crazy.'

'I agree.'

'Why did you say it if it wasn't true?'

She gave him a pitying look. 'Guess.'

'To get your own back?'

'Bull's-eye.' She took a deep breath. 'Goodbye.'

Patrick shook his head again. He felt stunned. After the way he'd battled with his conscience over coming here, it now seemed as if it had all been for nothing. Isobel wasn't pregnant. He wasn't going to have to deal with the consequences, arrange a trust fund, plan a schedule whereby he might see the child on a regular basis...

Or see Isobel on a regular basis, he acknowledged grimly. Now he came to think about it, he found it was incredibly difficult to separate one from the other, and the awareness that he had wanted to see her again made his response unnecessarily harsh.

'I suppose you enjoyed putting me on the spot,' he said coldly. 'Well, have a care, Miss Herriot. You may have forgotten, but I haven't. I still hold the lease on this shop, and I too am a vengeful man.'

Isobel didn't back down. 'Is that a threat, Mr Shannon?'

'No.' He was suddenly ashamed of even hinting at such a thing. 'I guess it was sour grapes, that's all.' He walked towards the door. 'Keep the shop.' His lips twisted. 'With my blessing.'

CHAPTER THIRTEEN

ISOBEL turned her car into Warwick Road and accelerated up to the gates of her parents' house. She would have parked in the drive, but she knew her father liked to keep it clear in case of any medical emergencies, and besides, she hoped whatever it was her mother wanted wouldn't take long.

Mrs Herriot was still hobbling around on her cast. But it was several weeks now since she had had the fall, and the plaster was hopefully coming off next week. Isobel would be glad when it did. It wasn't that she objected to helping her mother, but it was quite a strain trying to run the shop and make herself available whenever Mrs Herriot needed a lift or some shopping. She'd certainly been feeling more tired of late, and although the weather had turned cooler she was beginning to find it quite an effort to get up in the mornings.

Of course, she could guess why. Despite everything that had happened, she was still finding it difficult to get Patrick Riker—no, Shannon—out of her mind, and she knew it was going to take considerably longer than she had first anticipated to put that affair behind her.

She supposed it wasn't so unusual, really. She'd read that most women remembered their first lover, and the fact that she had been that much older when it happened was bound to play a part. But, she wondered, on those occasions when she was unable to keep the thoughts at bay, did most women remember the experience with such repugnance? How could he have done it? How could he have *used* her like that, and shown so little remorse afterwards?

With thoughts like these for company, it was no wonder she slept badly, she reflected now, getting out of the car and locking the door. And the knowledge that she wasn't being entirely honest with herself was no consolation.

However much she might try to wriggle out of it, the truth was that she had been as much to blame for what had happened as Patrick Shannon, and it was her own naïvety that was repugnant, nothing else.

Her mother was in the kitchen. When Isobel let herself into the house, Mrs Herriot called, 'I'm here, darling,' and her daughter walked with determined optimism in that direction. 'I'm just slicing some beans for supper,' the older woman added, somewhat unnecessarily. 'Help yourself to a cup of coffee.'

There was a jug of coffee keeping warm on its ring, but Isobel declined the invitation. In fact, the thought of coffee made her shudder and instead she helped herself to a glass of cold water from the dispenser in the fridge.

'Had a good day?' asked Mrs Herriot from her seat at the pine table. 'Mavis Tennant was telling me that her daughter's really thrilled that her pottery has proved so popular.'

'Is she?' Isobel propped her hips against the drainer and sipped from her glass. 'Well, it's good.' She paused. 'Was that what you wanted to tell me?'

Her mother gave her a wry look. 'Of course not. I'm sure you don't need me to tell you your business.'

'Thanks.' Isobel's tone was flat. 'So what is it?'

'Are you all right?'

Aware that her mother was watching her with concerned eyes, Isobel halted in the process of tipping her aching head back and flexed her shoulders. 'Of course. Why wouldn't I be?' She hesitated. 'I'm tired, that's all.'

'Tired?' Her mother regarded her sceptically. 'A girl like you shouldn't be tired. Why, when I was your age I was looking after two children and holding down a full-time job. You young people! You don't know you're born.'

Isobel had heard this argument before, and as if aware of the slight glazing of her daughter's eyes Mrs Herriot evidently decided she was wasting her time. 'Anyway,' she said, somewhat crossly, 'if you got out more you'd have less time to think about yourself. It's not hard work you're lacking, it's an active social life.'

'I know.'

Her mother blinked. This was a new response. 'You know?'

'Yes, I agree with you,' said Isobel evenly. 'I do need a social life. Maybe I ought to do something about getting one.'

'Like what?'

Her mother looked suspicious now, and Isobel allowed a faint smile to touch her lips. 'I'm just thinking that it might be a good idea to take some night classes this autumn,' she explained smoothly. 'I might even join the local operatic group, although I have to say singing has never been one of my strong points.'

'Oh!' Clearly, Mrs Herriot didn't know whether she was serious or not, and, deciding she had said as much as she could on the subject, she got up and rinsed the beans at the sink. 'Well...' she paused to give her next words more emphasis '... I've got some exciting news myself.'

'Have you?' Isobel knew a momentary pang. 'What is it?'

'Sit down and I'll tell you.'

Isobel sighed, but she did as she was told, and when they were both seated at the table Mrs Herriot divulged her news. 'You'll never believe it, but I've been invited to tender for the contract to redesign Foxworth Hall,' she announced proudly. 'What do you think about that?'

Isobel's mouth felt suddenly dry. 'Foxworth Hall?' she echoed faintly, but her mother was already hurrying on.

'When Mrs Foxworth died, most of the land and the commercial property was sold to Shannon Holdings. Well, I mean, I don't have to tell you that, do I? You already know that they're your new landlords, but at the time it was expected that the Foxworth family would hang onto the house and grounds. Anyway—' she adopted a confidential tone '—it appears that Patrick Shannon—you've heard of him, I'm sure—liked the area so much, he's persuaded the Foxworths to sell him the Hall as well.'

No!

Isobel's hand shook as she put the glass she was holding down on the table. It couldn't be true. Patrick wouldn't do that. He must know how it would make her feel. And to ask her own mother to tender for the work ... It was cruel.

'Are you sure you're all right, dear?' Despite her excitement at the unexpected opportunity she was being offered, Mrs Herriot had noticed Isobel's pale cheeks, and the film of sweat that was now beading on her forehead. 'Could you be sickening for something, do you think?'

'No.' Isobel managed a fairly convincing denial. 'It's just rather hot in here, Mum. Is the cooker on?'

'Well, it is.' Mrs Herriot glanced rather doubtfully behind her. 'But I had thought it was rather cool today.'

'Oh, well.' At all costs, Isobel wanted to divert her mother's attention from herself. 'It's probably me.' She licked her lips. 'Please go on.'

'If you're sure ...'

'I am.'

Isobel nodded, hoping the nausea she was feeling would soon subside, and Mrs Herriot, too excited at the prospect of tackling such a big project to pay more than cursory attention to her daughter, gave in.

'Where was I? Oh, yes. Mr Shannon himself has bought the Hall, and apparently he's quite keen to encourage local industry. In any event, his personal assistant has contacted several contractors in the area, and Herriot Designs was a natural choice for the interior decoration.'

A natural choice!

Isobel shivered now. It was no coincidence that Patrick had had his assistant contact Herriot Designs. She was fairly sure she had mentioned the fact that her mother was an interior decorator...

But her mother was talking again. 'I've heard that the house is in a pretty poor state of repair at the moment, which is probably why the Foxworths agreed to sell. It's going to need a small fortune spending on it, but I don't think that's going to bother Mr Shannon. He's not short of cash.'

She shook her head. 'It's hard to believe that when his grandfather left Ireland just after the last war and came to England he and his family were housed in a draughty old tenement in the East End of London.' Her expression was admiring. 'Of course, it was Patrick Shannon's father who started the company. He realised that all that derelict land that was going for a song in the fifties and sixties would eventually be worth a small fortune.'

Isobel's sickness wasn't abating. 'How do you know all this?' she protested weakly. 'Did you ask him?'

'Heavens, no. I haven't even seen the house yet, let alone met the owner!' exclaimed her mother impatiently. 'Your father found an article about Patrick Shannon in one of those business magazines he subscribes to. You know how journalists like to delve into a person's background and dig up facts that people would probably prefer to remain buried.' She grimaced. 'Anyway, it appears that he's really expanded the business since he took over, and Shannon Holdings is now an international concern. Isn't it wonderful?'

'For Patrick Shannon?'

'No. For me,' said her mother crossly. 'And for you. You never know, he may become one of your customers.'

'I hope not.'

Isobel knew she had to get out of there before she disgraced herself completely by throwing up in the sink. But when she pushed back her chair and got to her feet her mother gave her an aggrieved stare.

'I haven't finished.'

Isobel swallowed the bile that had collected at the back of her throat. 'Mum, I have to—'

'Whatever you have to do, it can wait five more minutes,' declared her mother tersely. She patted the seat of the chair where Isobel had been sitting. 'Please.'

Isobel didn't move. 'Well?'

Her mother suppressed her irritation with an obvious effort. 'Well, as you might expect, I do need to go and see the Hall—'

'No, Mum.'

'What do you mean, "No, Mum"? You don't know what I'm going to ask you yet.'

'I can guess.' Isobel gripped the back of the chair with desperate fingers. 'You want me to take you to Foxworth Hall.' She paused. 'Well, I can't.'

'Why can't you?'

'Because I can't, that's all.' Isobel pressed a hand to her burning throat. 'Get Daddy to take you.'

'Your father?' Mrs Herriot looked incredulous. 'He doesn't have the time to wait while I make a detailed examination of the premises. Have you any idea how long it can take? I could be there for several hours!'

'Then get him to drop you off and pick you up again afterwards,' said Isobel doggedly.

'And if he had an emergency in the meantime?' Her mother's expression was growing decidedly frosty. 'Am I supposed to hang about in an empty house until he finds the time to pick me up again?'

'You could phone.'

'The phone's still connected at the house, is it? You know that for a fact?'

Isobel shook her head. 'No.'

'So?' Mrs Herriot regarded her without expression. 'Do you still refuse to take me?'

'It's not a question of refusing—'

'Then what is it? It sounds remarkably like a refusal to me.'

'I—'

But before Isobel could say any more a door slammed in another part of the house, and presently Dr Herriot came into the room, stretching tired arms above his head.

'That's the last,' he said, referring to his surgery. 'Is there any coffee going?'

'On the ring,' said his wife with evident ill humour, and he gave Isobel a rather questioning look.

'Something wrong?'

'No—'

'What could be wrong?' interrupted his wife huffily. 'I've made our daughter a perfectly reasonable request, and she refuses even to—'

'Isobel?'

'Do we have another daughter?'

Dr Herriot ignored her. 'Isobel?' he said again. 'Are you all right? You're very pale.'

God! Isobel cringed. All she needed was for her father to start worrying about her health. She wanted no one digging into her recent history and discovering what a fool she'd made of herself. Particularly now...

'I'm tired, that's all,' she assured her father with assumed brightness. 'I—I was just explaining that I really don't have time to take Mum to Foxworth Hall. I know it's difficult for her at the moment, but—'

'You could always go on a Sunday,' suggested Dr Herriot with depressing reason. 'You don't open the shop on a Sunday, do you, Isobel?'

'No—'

'What a wonderful idea!'

Mrs Herriot's features underwent a miraculous change, and Isobel knew there was no way she was going to get out of this one.

'Unless there really is something you're not telling us,' added her father thoughtfully, and with a gesture of defeat Isobel gave in.

'All right,' she said, wishing she didn't feel so resentful of her mother's triumphant air. 'What time on Sunday? I—I had planned to do some stocktaking in the morning.'

'Could you pick me up at half past two?'

'Half past two?' Isobel managed a controlled nod. 'But now I've got to go.'

She had to stop the car halfway home, the nausea she had managed to subdue at her parents' house finally overwhelming her. Luckily there was a convenient hedgerow where she could conceal herself from the occasional vehicle that used this short cut, which was little wider than a bridleway, and when she eventually crawled back into the car she was near to tears.

It wasn't fair, she thought unhappily. Patrick Shannon had no right to do this to her. Not only was he moving into the area, which up until now she'd regarded as her refuge, but he had also deliberately involved her mother in his machinations, knowing how humiliated it would make her feel.

She heaved a trembling sigh. Was this his way of punishing her for lying to him, or was she getting things completely out of perspective? His decision to buy Foxworth Hall might have been made months ago. Was she being absurdly conceited in thinking that anything she'd done might have influenced his plans? Probably. But the suspicion that there was more to it than pure chance would not go away.

CHAPTER FOURTEEN

'ISN'T it magnificent?'

Mrs Herriot stood leaning on the cane she used to get about, gazing up at the vaulted ceiling that arched at least forty feet above their heads. For all the roof was grimy and in obvious need of attention, its lines were undeniably symmetrical.

'It looks dirty to me,' replied Isobel dampeningly, determined not to like anything about the old mansion. She hadn't wanted to come here, and she certainly hadn't wanted to stay while her mother made her inspection. She supposed she should be grateful that the place was deserted. At least Patrick had had the good sense to stay away.

'Well, of course it's dirty!' exclaimed her mother irritably. 'I doubt if it's been touched for years. Mrs Foxworth was an old woman, and by all accounts she wasn't the easiest person to get along with. Her family seldom visited her, and I suppose the place just fell into disrepair.'

Isobel glanced about her. 'Are you sure you're going to be able to handle this, Mum?' she asked with more warmth. 'It looks pretty daunting to me.'

'I suppose it is daunting,' agreed her mother, nodding. 'But it's also a challenge, and I'm looking forward to it. After all, I'm only to be employed to design colour schemes and fabrics. An architect will have to decide if any structural repairs are needed.'

Isobel regarded her doubtfully. 'I thought you'd be expected to find the tradesmen too,' she remarked. 'Doesn't—' the name stuck in her throat 'doesn't Mr Shannon want the whole package?'

'Perhaps.' Her mother moistened her lips and moved across to the fireplace, running an exploratory finger along the dusty mantel. 'What I meant was, I shan't be expected to get up on a ladder and varnish the beams myself.'

Isobel shrugged. In her opinion, her mother was biting off rather more than she could chew in tendering for the Foxworth contract. Herriot Designs was a successful little operation, but it was *little*. From what Isobel could see, a team of designers was needed here, with a veritable army of tradespeople to follow on.

'I think I'll start upstairs,' said Mrs Herriot now, making for the fan-shaped staircase that gave access to the upper floors. A flight of shallow steps led up to a central landing, before dividing into two halves to sweep up to the gallery above. She tucked her notebook under her arm. 'Are you coming?'

Isobel hesitated. 'You go ahead,' she said, seemingly uninterested. The last thing she wanted to do was see where Patrick was going to sleep. Was he buying this house for himself, or was he planning to get married? she wondered. Or was it just another property? Somewhere he could invite his business associates, with hunting and fishing thrown in?

Mrs Herriot pulled a wry face and started up the carpeted staircase. Although the house had been emptied of much of its furniture, the floor coverings still remained. Isobel guessed that no one had been keen to lift the heavy woollen broadloom for fear of what it might be concealing. If it hadn't been lifted for years, there could be bugs—or even dry rot—lurking underneath.

She waited until her mother reached the galleried landing, and then, when Mrs Herriot disappeared through another door, she turned and strolled into the room that opened off the hall to her right.

She found herself in another huge chamber, but this time its size was moderated somewhat by the tall, folding doors, which could be used to divide the apartment into two much more manageable rooms. The doors stood open at present, and the carpet was littered with scraps of paper and catalogues, and the marks left by half a dozen rows of wooden chairs. She had heard that the furniture had been auc-

tioned, and she guessed that this was where the sale had
taken place. It made the room look rather sad and neglected.
She didn't like to think of the old lady's home being broken
up.

She walked to the long windows and looked out.
Although the panes were grimy, the view from the house
was obviously a large selling point. The ground fell away
for some distance beyond the terrace, allowing an uninter-
rupted view of Horsham Vale. She could even see the spire
of St Stephen's church at Swalford, and the river winding
through the valley, on its way to meet the Avon.

The land immediately surrounding the Hall had been sold
with the house, which meant that there were several acres
of fields and paddocks beyond the more formal gardens
that encircled the house. Not that there was much to choose
between them at the moment, Isobel reflected wryly. Like
everything else, the garden had been neglected, and the
shrubbery was a jungle of overgrown plants.

It was so quiet, too. If she hadn't known for a fact that
her mother was upstairs, she could have been forgiven for
believing that she was completely alone. Unlike at the
cottage, any creaking floorboards were too far away to be
noticed, and it was only the sound of a door slamming that
obliged her to go and see how Mrs Herriot was getting on.

She came out into the hall again, and then came to an
abrupt halt. So much for Patrick's considering anyone's
feelings but his own, she thought bitterly as the man she
had hoped never to have to see again shed his leather jacket
into a stone niche beside the hearth. He wasn't yet aware
of her presence, and she guessed that while she had been
admiring the view from the rear windows he must have
driven up to the front door. He had to have seen her car,
but had he recognised it? She wondered if he had expected
her mother to be here alone.

Her heart hammered in her chest. In black jeans and a
collarless chambray shirt, he was just as dangerous to her
peace of mind. Suppressing the sense of panic that rose
inside her at the thought of speaking to him, she considered
stepping back into the room behind her. She could let him

go upstairs, let him talk to her mother. It would be easier to face him with a third party present.

But even as the idea surfaced he turned and saw her standing in the open doorway. '*God!*' he said sharply, and she saw, somewhat to her satisfaction, that he had received a shock too. 'What are you doing here?' he added, loosening his collar and coming towards her. He cast a glance about him. 'Did curiosity get the better of you? I never thought you'd come here without being coerced.'

Did he think she was here through choice?

Her anger simmering, Isobel gave him a filthy look. 'My mother still can't drive,' she told him tersely. 'She doesn't get the cast off her foot until next week.'

'Ah.' Patrick conceded his mistake, and then, lifting his hand, he brushed his knuckles against her mouth. 'You don't forgive very easily, do you, Belle? Heaven forbid that I should have thought you'd come to see me.'

Isobel jerked back, dashing his hand away—like some outraged spinster in a B movie, she was to think with some irritation later. 'I didn't know you'd be here. I understood from my mother that the agent had lent her the keys.'

'That's right.' Patrick ignored her instinctive recoil and thrust his hands into the back pockets of his jeans. Rocking back on his heels, he did as her mother had done earlier and surveyed the ceiling. 'God, I hope she knows what she's taking on.'

Isobel frowned. She had determined not to get into a conversation with him, but that remark was so provocative, she had to ask, 'My mother hasn't got the contract yet, has she?' She flushed as his eyes returned to her face. 'I understood she was just—well, tendering for the job.'

Patrick regarded her consideringly. 'How have you been, Belle?' he asked, without answering her question. 'You know, I think you've lost weight. Have you been working too hard?'

Isobel forced herself to breathe evenly, even though every breath was an effort. He was being deliberately obtuse—a habit he had honed to perfection. Why couldn't she treat him as casually, instead of suffering this intense sense of awareness every time he was near?

'My mother's upstairs,' she said at last, copying his lack of candour. 'As she's probably heard your arrival, perhaps you ought to go and introduce yourself to—'

'You didn't.'

Isobel looked blank. 'I didn't what?'

'Hear my arrival,' he replied pleasantly, and she gave him an impatient look.

'That's because I was at the back of the house,' she retorted, only realising after the words had been uttered that she had admitted she'd been looking around.

And he noticed. 'So, do you like it?' he asked, his green eyes disturbingly intent, and Isobel decided she had little to gain now by being dishonest.

'It needs a lot doing to it,' she prevaricated, with a careless shrug. 'I suppose the structure is passable. You certainly have a beautiful view.'

'Do I?'

Patrick's lips twitched, and once again she realised what she'd inadvertently implied. 'From the windows,' she appended tersely. 'That's what I was doing through there.' She indicated the room behind her. 'There's nothing much to admire indoors.'

'I wouldn't say that,' remarked Patrick, sidestepping her and strolling into the huge drawing room, so that she couldn't be sure if he was being facetious again or not. 'I know it needs a lot of renovation. And I dare say it's going to cost an arm and a leg to put it right. But I'm fortunate enough to be able to afford it, and at the end of the day I'll have a comfortable home where I can entertain my friends and family.'

Isobel took a deep breath. She would not follow him, she told herself grimly. But when he spoke again she found herself listening, and eventually moving to hover in the open doorway.

'They had the sale in here,' he was saying, confirming what she had suspected before. He dug his booted heel into the carpet where one of the wooden chairs had left a mark. 'You didn't attend.'

'Me?' Isobel gave a bemused snort. 'Of course not.'

'I thought you might,' he said lifting his head from an examination of the carpet and giving her a penetrating look. 'I was here.' He paused. 'Didn't Richard tell you?'

'Richard?' She stared at him with cold accusation in her eyes. 'Is that why you've come here? To find out if I'm still seeing Richard?'

'Of course not.' He was impatient now, and she sensed he hadn't meant to ask her that. 'I didn't know you were here until you appeared like a wraith in the doorway. It was your mother I came to see, as you well know.'

'Then why don't you go and see her?' demanded Isobel crossly, aware that for all her supposed indifference to this man he could still get under her skin. 'She'll be wondering why I'm holding you up.'

His eyes narrowed. 'She doesn't know we know one another, I take it?'

'You take it right,' said Isobel sarcastically. 'Why would I mention you to her? I prefer to keep my mistakes to myself.'

'Was it a mistake?' He gazed at her with sudden intensity. 'I seem to recall we were rather good together.' He paused. 'You seemed to think so too at the time.'

Isobel caught her breath. 'I suppose that's your excuse for everything, is it? So long as you're happy, to hell with anyone else's feelings. It hasn't occurred to you that I might object to you bringing it up again, has it? You're completely self-centred. You don't care about anyone but yourself.'

'Whoa!' Patrick made a pretence of being rocked by her tirade, but his tone was less than humorous when he made his reply. 'Forgive me for being frank, but I'm only telling it how it was. I can't help it if you don't like the truth.'

'And when has the truth ever bothered you?' countered Isobel heatedly. 'Except when you were afraid I'd called your bluff.' She took a calming breath, and then continued wearily, 'What are you doing here, Patrick? Why have you bought this house? Does it bug you so much that I can resist your charms?'

His eyes darkened angrily. 'Have a care, Belle—'

'No. *You* have a care—'

'Isobel?'

Mrs Herriot's puzzled voice broke into their exchange, and Isobel realised, to her horror, that while they had been arguing her mother had come downstairs. She must have heard Patrick's car, after all, and now she was standing just behind her daughter, looking anxious. How much had she heard? Isobel fretted, aware that her throat was unpleasantly dry. She hoped her nerves would not let her down in this situation. She wanted no spurious sympathy from Patrick Shannon.

'You must be Mrs Herriot.' With the supreme self-confidence that only moments before Isobel had been berating him for possessing, Patrick saved her from any immediate explanation. As the younger woman moved aside, he held out his hand in greeting. 'How do you do? I'm Patrick Shannon. I understand from your daughter that you've been looking around the house.'

Mrs Herriot still looked perplexed, but this was the man she was hoping would employ her services and, forcing a professional smile to her mouth, she shook his hand. 'How do you do, Mr Shannon? Yes, I've been attempting to assess what's required.' She cast a doubtful glance in Isobel's direction, and then continued smoothly, 'I expect you realise it will be some time before I can start work?'

'Yes.' Patrick nodded. 'I realise that.' He paused. 'But I understand you were eager to look around the property. I suppose the sooner you see the actual rooms, the more time you have to estimate the work involved.'

Isobel said nothing. There was nothing for her to say, after all, and while Patrick and her mother continued their discussion she just stood there, feeling hopelessly out of place. She knew that her mother was not going to accept Patrick's explanation at face value. Whatever she'd heard, it had clearly not been an argument about the house.

They were discussing the bathrooms that needed to be installed, and whether it was psychosomatic or not Isobel wasn't sure, but suddenly she wanted to use one rather desperately. If only she'd told her mother she'd come back for her in an hour she might have avoided this meeting altogether.

'I—I wonder...' she began, breaking into a debate about the advantages of keeping the fretwork screens that hid the old iron radiators, and her mother gave her a chilling look.

'Yes?'

'Um—' Isobel strove for an excuse. 'As you've got—um—Mr Shannon here to keep you company, would you mind if I came back in, say, an hour?'

'Oh, Isobel!'

Mrs Herriot was evidently put out, but again Patrick came to the rescue. 'I can drop your mother back home,' he declared at once, earning that lady's relieved gratitude.

'Oh, if you would...'

'No problem,' he assured her smoothly, but Isobel had the unwilling suspicion that she shouldn't leave him and her mother together.

'Well, it's very kind of you, of course...' she began, trying to hide her chagrin, but her mother seemed to take it as read.

'I'll speak to you later, Isobel,' she said over her shoulder, hobbling across the room to examine a patch of damp on a far wall. 'Drive carefully.'

'I'll see you out.'

Patrick fell into step beside her as she started towards the main door, and although she would have liked to tell him to get lost she was obliged to suffer his company in silence. But she resented the way he had used her tentative withdrawal to his own advantage.

She felt better outside. It was probably her imagination, but the air didn't seem so oppressive, and the knowledge that she could get into her car and drive away was an enormous relief.

The Bentley, its chauffeur leaning on the bonnet, was parked just behind her modest Peugeot. Joe—wasn't that

the name Patrick had used?—lifted a languid hand in
greeting, and she thought how delighted her mother was
going to be, at being driven home in such style. She just
wished she knew what game Patrick was playing. She
couldn't believe he really wanted to employ Herriot Designs.

She hadn't locked the car, but before she could reach out
and open the door herself Patrick pre-empted her. With his
muscular frame wedged between the open door and the car,
there was no way she could get round him, unless she wanted
to cause the kind of scene that his chauffeur would surely
enjoy.

'Have dinner with me tonight.'

Isobel gasped. 'In your dreams!'

'That too,' he conceded in a low voice. 'Come on. I want
to talk to you. I want to explain why—why I did what I
did.'

'Get out of my way.'

Isobel was in no mood to be polite. To add to her worries,
a feeling of faintness was sweeping over her. If she didn't
sit down soon, she might expose her weakness to him.

'What are you afraid of?' As if he was aware that they
had an audience too, Patrick half turned so that his back
was to the chauffeur. 'For God's sake, Belle, stop being so
childish! I want to see you again. Is that so unacceptable?'

'Frankly, yes.'

'Because you're afraid of me.'

'Dammit, I am not afraid of you!'

But she was. As she stood there, steeling herself not to
show any emotion, she acknowledged that she was shaking
in her boots. She was afraid of the power he had over her,
of the ability he possessed to make her betray herself.

'Then have dinner with me.'

Isobel took a deep breath. 'Can't you understand? I don't
want to have dinner with you.'

Patrick's mouth hardened. 'I'm afraid I'm going to have
to insist.'

She swayed. 'Insist?'

It was meant to sound incredulous, but the tremor in her
voice rather spoiled the effect.

'Yes, insist,' agreed Patrick flatly. 'Tonight or tomorrow; it's your choice. Now, do we have an agreement?'

Isobel stared disbelievingly at him. 'Or—or my mother will lose this contract? Is that what you're saying?'

'No!' His denial was savage, and he gazed at her as if he'd like to wring her neck for suggesting such a thing. But then, as if one idea had spawned another, his lips twisted. 'Or I'll close your bloody shop down,' he appended harshly. 'There. Is that what you wanted to hear?'

CHAPTER FIFTEEN

HE'D got his way—but at what price?

As the Peugeot sped recklessly away down the drive, Patrick stood and watched it go with a brooding introspection. Dammit, why did she do this to him? Why did she make him feel like the world's biggest heel, just because he wanted to see her again? For God's sake, she ought to be flattered. He knew any number of women who would be happy to take her place.

No, he was not short of friends—or dates either, he conceded grimly, even if he hadn't responded to any of the messages Joanna had left on his machine. Evidently she had thought better of her outburst, but he was cynically aware that his money could conceal a million flaws.

Was that why Isobel didn't want to know him? Because she saw the flaws in him? Certainly the fact that he was the chairman of one of the top five hundred companies in the world meant nothing to her. Indeed, he was fairly sure she'd have regarded him more favourably if he had been the salesman Richard had pretended to be.

The trouble was, he had deceived her, and it seemed she couldn't—or wouldn't—forgive him for that. So why did he have this desperate need to justify himself to her? Why did he care whether she hated him or not?

'Sexy lady!'

Joe's careless comment reminded him that the other man had been a witness to the whole sorry fiasco, and what he said made Patrick's anger swell. Isobel wasn't some bimbo to be described in such terms, and he also found he didn't like the idea that another man might recognise her appeal.

'Leave it,' he said, those two words encompassing such a wealth of hostility that Joe put up his hands in mock defence.

136

'Hey, no sweat, boss,' he said, but there was a note of disappointment in his voice and Patrick's face assumed a rueful look.

'Yeah, yeah, I know,' he muttered. 'I'm sorry. I guess you caught me in a filthy mood.'

'I'd say,' agreed Joe, with some relief. 'Wasn't that—?' He broke off, and then, seeing that his employer was waiting for him to finish, he mumbled, 'Isobel Herriot? Forgive me if I sound dumb, but I thought that was over.'

Patrick's hands balled in his pockets. 'You thought what was over?' he enquired in a controlled tone, and Joe seemed to realise that once again he had overstepped the mark.

'It doesn't matter,' he said, hauling open the door to the Bentley and surveying the interior of the car. 'Will you be much longer, or do you want me to take a hike too?'

'For your information, there never was a—*relationship* between Isobel and Richard,' Patrick told him harshly. 'Does that answer your question?'

Joe pulled a lugubrious face. 'Let me know when you want to leave, huh?' he suggested, settling himself behind the wheel. 'Hey, I'm just the chauffeur. I don't know nothin'!'

Patrick's lips twitched. They both knew that Joe was not *just* a chauffeur. They'd been together too long, shared too many experiences for Patrick to regard him as anything less than a friend. But in this instance Patrick was vulnerable, and it was not a feeling he could share.

In his absence, Isobel's mother had progressed into the dining room, and when Patrick found her she was poking her pencil into some plaster that was crumbling away from the skirting board. He wondered what she was thinking—whether she found it strange that he should have taken so long when all he was supposed to have been doing was escorting her daughter to the door.

But when she looked up and saw him her first concern was for the house. 'It looks as though, when this paper comes off, it will bring all the plaster with it,' she said. 'I'm afraid that's true of all the rooms I've inspected so far. You're looking at a major plastering job.'

Patrick forced himself to concentrate on what she was saying. He'd noticed that some of the paper was peeling, but the mechanics of what he was taking on were not really his concern. 'Do you think I'm mad?' he asked as she made another annotation in her notebook, and Mrs Herriot permitted him a cautious look.

'Of course not,' she said. 'Basically, the house is sound, and I'm sure that when all the renovations are completed you'll have a home to be proud of.'

'A home to be proud of.' Patrick repeated her words rather cynically, but if Mrs Herriot noticed she chose not to take him up on it.

'You're lucky,' she added. 'You won't have to live in the house while the tradesmen are working. Some people have no option. It's the only home they own.'

Patrick considered what she'd said. 'And do you think it's wrong? Owning more than one house?'

'Heavens, no.' She was serenely adamant about that. 'I just wondered—well, why you chose to buy Foxworth Hall, Mr Shannon. If it's not an impertinent suggestion, there must be many more suitable properties than this.'

'Perhaps.' Patrick inclined his head. 'But this is the house I wanted.'

'Because you bought the rest of the Foxworth estate?'

'Because I like the area,' replied Patrick, his tone hardening a little. He was prepared to accept that as Isobel's mother she might be curious about their relationship, but his reasons for buying Foxworth weren't even clear in his own mind yet.

'Do you know the area well?'

Patrick's lips thinned. 'Reasonably.' He surveyed the room, with its gloomy purple wallpaper and crumbling plaster, with an impatient eye. 'I'll leave you to it,' he added curtly. 'Let me know when you're ready to leave.'

She came to find him perhaps an hour later.

After another examination of the hall had convinced him that he was not making the biggest mistake of his life, Patrick had gone to ground in the orangery, finding an abandoned canvas chair and giving himself over to introspection.

The afternoon had changed as he'd sat there, one ankle propped across his knee, his eyes fixed on the spire of the distant church. It had been overcast earlier, but it had soon started to rain, and the pattering drops had provided a barrier between himself and the world beyond these walls.

'Mr Shannon?'

The sound of Isobel's mother's cane tapping on the ground should have warned him of her approach, but it hadn't. Patrick started almost guiltily to his feet when she spoke his name, aware that he'd forgotten she was here.

'Mrs Herriot,' he answered, forcing a polite smile to his lips. 'I'm sorry. I was daydreaming. Are you ready to go?'

'I think so.' Her smile was also forced. 'If it's not an imposition.' She paused. 'I suppose you could always call me a taxi. I'm sure you must carry one of those mobile phones.'

'I won't hear of it,' he assured her gallantly, wondering somewhat wryly if she'd still be as polite if she knew what he had been thinking about when she'd disturbed him. The heated images of himself and Isobel tangled in the sheets of her bed were as unwelcome to him as they would have been to her, but he couldn't escape them. 'Have you got all the information you need?'

'I think so.' But something about the way she said it, alerted him to the fact that she wasn't happy. 'However, I'm afraid you may have to find yourself another interior designer.'

Patrick frowned. 'You don't think you can handle it?' He shrugged. 'I realise it's probably bigger than anything you've tackled this far, and perhaps you're concerned about the initial outlay—'

'It's not that.'

'No?'

'No.' She shifted a little uncomfortably.

'My assistant did explain that it would be some time before the architect—'

'I just don't think it would be—appropriate for me to tender for the contract,' she interrupted him stiffly, and Patrick suppressed an oath.

'Appropriate?' He stared at her. 'What the h—what are you talking about?'

Mrs Herriot pursed her lips before speaking. 'I'm not a fool, Mr Shannon. It's evident that you—that you and Isobel are—acquainted. And I'd rather not take a job that I've only been offered out of charity.'

'Out of charity?' Patrick was impatient with himself for repeating everything she said, but he couldn't help it. 'I don't know what you mean.'

'Oh, come along, Mr Shannon. I know my daughter, and it was obvious when I came downstairs that you and she were—well, arguing. I suppose Isobel told you about my little accident, and you thought you'd help me out by offering me this opportunity—'

'It wasn't like that.' Patrick could feel himself getting irritated, and he didn't like the feeling. Particularly not in the present circumstances. 'You obviously don't know your daughter well enough if you think she'd ask me for anything!'

Mrs Herriot frowned. 'So you didn't know we were related?'

'I didn't say that.' Patrick gave an inward groan at her expression. He didn't need this. 'But you have to believe me when I say that she had no part in my decision to use—local expertise.'

Mrs Herriot looked sceptical, and he didn't blame her. 'Then what were you arguing about?' she asked.

Patrick was staggered now. 'I think that's our business, don't you?' he replied pleasantly. 'Let me show you out.'

Joe had been dozing, but he sprang out of the car at their approach, opening the rear door with exaggerated ceremony. 'Horsham, sir?' he enquired of Patrick, adopting a deferential air, and his employer gave him a warning look.

'The lady will give you the address,' he agreed, stepping back instead of joining Isobel's mother in the car. 'Pick me up later,' he added in an undertone. Then, lifting a hand in farewell, he turned back into the house.

A couple of hours later, after a shower, a shave and a change of clothes, Patrick felt a little better. He'd booked himself and Joe into the Stratford Moat House, and it was amazing how much more optimistic dealing with ordinary people had made him feel.

By the time he pulled up outside Isobel's cottage, he was almost prepared to believe that the evening might be a success. After all, it wasn't as if either of them were children, and if he was honest with her she might even begin to understand.

The muscles in his stomach tightened. Who was he kidding? It wasn't the fact that he thought he owed Isobel an explanation that had persuaded him to buy Foxworth Hall. Nor was the need to soothe her feelings the sole thing that kept him awake nights, and prevented him from resuming his relationship with Joanna. Dammit, she knew why he'd gone to see her; she'd guessed that Jillian was behind his little charade. Why couldn't she try to understand his feelings, and let their association move on to something else?

But on to what else?

As he pushed open the car door and got out, he was unwillingly aware that he didn't know the answer to that. All he really knew was that he wanted—no, *needed*—to see her, and that buying Foxworth Hall had seemed to provide the means.

Despite what he'd told Mrs Herriot, he had had his assistant contact Herriot Designs deliberately. When he'd been making his preliminary enquiries into Isobel's background, he'd discovered then that her mother was in business for herself, but of course he hadn't expected to show his hand so soon. It had been just his bad luck that Isobel had had to chauffeur her mother that afternoon, and a continuation of that same fortune that had caused Mrs Herriot to come upon them as she had.

Having met Isobel's mother, however, he had realised she was nothing like her daughter. He couldn't imagine Isobel coming right out and asking if he was involved with her daughter. Besides, he and Isobel weren't involved, he reminded himself, releasing the catch on the garden gate and starting up the path. He had no intention of getting involved with anyone who took their relationship so seriously. So why the hell didn't he just cut his losses and run?

The door opened as he reached the porch, and he realised she must have been watching for him. But not for any charitable reason, he impressed upon himself severely. He guessed she was afraid he might try to make love to her again.

She used the excuse of locking the door to turn her back on him, thus giving them both a breathing space, and Patrick started down the path again, thinking that there was no point in beginning the evening with harsh words.

In any case, he was unhappily aware of the way his emotions made a mockery of his reasoning. Even though they hadn't parted on the best of terms that afternoon, he knew now that he had been impatient to see her again. Although the brief look she had shared with him had hardly been friendly, he was pathetically eager to put their differences behind them.

She was wearing the dress she had worn the evening she had had dinner with Richard, and he wondered if it was a deliberate attempt to remind him of that inglorious occasion. Whatever, its softly draped bodice and narrow, ankle-length skirt were very feminine, the colour—a sort of muted bronze—going well with the long navy linen jacket she wore over it.

The colour also matched her hair, which she had scraped back into the thick braid she wore for work. Another statement? he wondered wryly, holding the gate so that she could precede him through it. He sighed. Why was he here? he asked himself. Why was he doing this? Was she really worth the trouble? Or was he temporarily off his head?

She didn't speak, and, realising he wasn't prepared to spend the evening in a hostile silence, he deliberately sought her eyes as he opened the Bentley's passenger door. 'I'm sorry for what happened this afternoon,' he said. 'I'm not usually such an unpleasant bastard. Put it down to pure frustration.'

'I doubt if there's anything pure about you, Mr Shannon,' retorted Isobel sharply, getting into the car. And then, as if it was all too much trouble to continue fencing with him, she tipped her head back against the soft leather squabs. 'Besides, I dare say you got your come-uppance with my mother.' Her lips tilted. 'She's not usually so restrained, I have to admit.'

Patrick grinned as he folded his length into the seat beside her. 'No.' He nodded. 'I'd say that was the understatement of the year.' He paused, wondering if he should go on, and then decided to take a chance. 'She suggested you'd recommended her for the job.'

CHAPTER SIXTEEN

ISOBEL gasped. 'She didn't!'

'She did.' Patrick started the engine. 'She'd come to the conclusion that you and I must be involved.'

'Oh, God!'

Isobel pressed an uneasy hand to her stomach. She had suspected something like that might happen, but it was infinitely more disturbing to hear that she had been right. Mrs Herriot could always be relied upon to do the unexpected, though her daughter had hoped she might be more discreet in this case.

Even so, she hadn't answered the phone since she got back to the cottage. It had rung several times, and she knew now that her mother must be desperate to get in touch with her. If she'd been able to drive her own car, she would have come to see her. She would probably blame Isobel for that, too.

'Anyway, she's decided she can't take the commission in the circumstances,' went on Patrick. 'I'm afraid we didn't part on the best of terms.'

Isobel blinked. 'Why not?' She licked her lips. 'You didn't tell her—'

'That I'd slept with her daughter?' Patrick gave her a wry smile. 'Give me a break! That's exactly the kind of topic to discuss with your girlfriend's mother! How should I have put it? Oh, yes, by the way, I seduced Isobel in June, but I haven't seen her since.'

Isobel felt hot colour invade her cheeks. 'I'm not your girlfriend.'

'No, you're not,' he conceded a little flatly, and Isobel wished she hadn't said that and evoked such a denial. 'And I suppose I have seen you since then, if you must be pedantic. A couple of times, by my calculation. Not that they

144

were particularly memorable occasions. It might be easier if we could just put the past behind us.'

'But we can't, can we?' Isobel was curt, but she couldn't help it. 'I know you probably think I'm absurdly sensitive, but I don't like the idea of being used. Even if you did think Richard and I were having an affair, did you have to prove we weren't in such a drastic way?'

'Yes!' Patrick's reply was unexpectedly passionate, and she noticed the way his knuckles whitened on the wheel. 'Can't you get it through your head that I didn't take you to bed just to please my sister? For God's sake, I wanted you!' He paused. 'I still do.'

Isobel swallowed. 'I don't believe you.'

'Isn't that my line?' His lips twisted with sudden irony. 'What is it with you, Belle? Why should you think it isn't true?'

'Because...'

But she didn't really have an answer. Except that the knowledge frightened her with its subtle statement of intent.

'What about that woman?'

'What woman?'

Isobel pursed her lips. 'The woman you were having dinner with. Your *real* girlfriend.'

'Joanna?'

'If that's her name.'

'What about her?' He sounded perplexed. 'Joanna has no claim on me.'

'Hasn't she?' Isobel was suspicious. 'She seemed to think she had. Don't tell me you haven't slept with her, because I won't believe you.'

Patrick sighed. 'I don't think my relationship with Joanna has any part in this discussion,' he said impatiently, forced to concentrate on the traffic as they turned onto the Stratford road. 'All right. We've been friends for years, but she doesn't control my life.'

'You have an—open—relationship?' Isobel was bitter, and it showed.

'Do you have a problem with that?' he asked tightly, and she sensed he resented her asking him these questions. 'As

a matter of fact, as of that evening at the club, we don't
have a relationship. Now can we talk about something else?'

'Why?' Isobel had to know. 'Because talking about—her
is upsetting to you?'

'No, dammit.' He swore. 'Quite the opposite, actually.'
He cast her a fulminating look. 'Have you seen Richard
again?'

Isobel's lips parted. 'No!'

Her denial was indignant, but Patrick seemed unmoved
by her outraged response. 'What's wrong?' he asked. 'Don't
you like your own medicine?'

'That's not the same thing.'

'Why isn't it?'

Isobel swallowed. 'Because Richard and I were never—
I just *knew* him, that's all.' She bent her head. 'As your
representative, I suppose.'

'Hmm.' Patrick mulled this over. 'But you knew he was
married. You mentioned his daughter on the first occasion
we met.'

'Susannah?' Isobel shrugged. 'Yes. But he said he and
his wife were having problems. He'd asked me to go out
with him several times before I gave in.'

Patrick glanced her way. 'And why did you give in?'

'That's none of your business.' Isobel's response was
suddenly indignant, and she was aware that she had been
in danger of confiding in him. She lifted her head. 'Perhaps
I'd had a bad experience. Perhaps I wanted reassurance.'
Her lips twisted. 'In the event, I didn't get it, did I?'

'I suppose it depends what kind of reassurance you were
seeking,' replied Patrick obliquely. 'If it's any consolation,
I was seeking the same.'

'You?' Isobel was derisive. 'You don't need reassurance.
You're superbly in control of events. You don't do anything you don't want to do.'

Patrick's teeth ground together. 'How do you know that?
Do you have a private line to my innermost feelings? Because let me tell you you couldn't be more wrong.'

'Why?'

'Why?' He glared at her. 'Because if I could control my feelings I wouldn't be here. I don't like what you do to me any more than you like what I do to you.'

Isobel caught her breath. 'I don't know what you mean.'

'Yes, you do.' Patrick sounded weary now. 'All right, let me lay it out for you. You guessed I'd come to see you because Jillian asked me to.'

'Jillian?'

'My sister,' said Patrick tautly. 'Richard's wife? The wife he was supposedly at odds with?'

'Supposedly?'

'Yes. Yes.' He repeated himself because she looked so disbelieving. 'Richard and Jill have had problems from the start,' he conceded, 'but Jill always forgives him, and Richard doesn't want a divorce.'

'You're saying I'm not the first woman he's—'

'Had a relationship with?' broke in Patrick shortly. 'No.'

'It was hardly a relationship.'

'I accept that.' They had reached the outskirts of Stratford, and Patrick had to concentrate on getting into the right lane for the city centre. 'But who knows what might have happened if I hadn't intervened?' he added as they cleared the junction.

'Nothing would have happened,' declared Isobel hotly. 'It may come as something of a surprise to you, but I was not desperate to—to...'

'Lose your virginity?' suggested Patrick softly, and her face flamed.

'Sleep with a man,' she amended tersely. 'And don't you think you ought to tell me where we're going? I assumed we'd be going to Swalford again.'

'I thought we might try a restaurant I know near the river,' responded Patrick easily, slowing once again to negotiate the bottleneck at the foot of the high street. He indicated right, and turned into the multi-storey car park. 'We can walk from here. It isn't very far.'

It was still light when they emerged into the flow of human traffic. It was the height of the tourist season, although the crowds who flocked to see Shakespeare's birthplace seemed to come at all times of the year. Obviously, it was busier in the summer, when people could take the open-air bus tours, or saunter happily beside the river, soaking up the Elizabethan charm of the place. But even in winter the Bard had his faithful band of followers, visiting the theatres or shopping in the town.

Isobel hoped she wouldn't see anyone she knew as she and Patrick made their way across the bridge and up the street that ran parallel with the main thoroughfare. It wasn't that she was ashamed of being seen with him. On the contrary, she was not unaware that his dark masculinity attracted several interested glances from women who were in groups or on their own. But she would prefer not to have to make introductions. How did you introduce a man you knew next to nothing about in one way, and intimately in another?

And it was the knowledge of that intimacy that kept the blood racing through her veins and her nerves on edge. He didn't touch her as they walked, but she was overwhelmingly aware of him beside her. He was wearing a navy suit this evening with a matching silk shirt beneath. But although his collar was buttoned he wasn't wearing a tie, and she imagined she could see the dark shadow of hair that arrowed down below his belt.

She couldn't stop thinking about that evening at the cottage. She didn't want to think about it, but somehow she couldn't get it out of her mind. When she thought he wasn't looking, she cast faintly anxious looks in his direction. It seemed so incredible that they had ever been that close.

Had he really undressed her? Had he really cupped her breasts in his hands, and suckled them with his tongue? Had he slid his hands down over her hips, and then between her legs, parting her softness for his invasion? Oh, God, she thought, she was arousing herself, and he hadn't even taken her hand.

He looked at her then, meeting her eyes when she least expected it and seeing the disturbing awareness in her face. Without a word, he gripped her wrist and pulled her to

walk beside him. 'For God's sake, don't look at me like
that,' he said thickly. 'Not when I can't do anything about
it.'

Isobel came to her senses with a start. In heaven's name
what was she thinking of? With a jerky little movement,
she pulled herself free and moved ahead of him. This
evening was not going to end the way the other one had.
She was definitely sure of that.

They ate at a restaurant that Isobel had previously only
heard of by reputation. It was small, and discreet, but evidently popular, judging by the queue of people outside
waiting for a table. Patrick, however, had no hesitation in
forging his way to the front. Despite her belief that he was
a newcomer to the district, he apparently knew the form
and had booked ahead.

And, although she'd been sure she would find the rest
of the evening a strain, Patrick was so skilful, he soon had
her discussing her plans for the shop. When he wasn't
teasing her or embarrassing her, he was amazingly good
company. But she'd known that already. That was how he
had inveigled his way into her life.

It was only when their eyes met that she saw something
less innocent glittering in his. Whatever his lips were saying,
his eyes held an entirely different message, and she found
herself emptying her wineglass far more often than she
would have liked.

The food was delicious—what she ate of it. She had invited Patrick to choose her meal, too nervous when they'd
first sat down to give any serious attention to the menu,
and a hot mousse of crab and lobster was followed by slices
of roast duckling in an orange sauce. There was rice pudding
for dessert—a choice that Patrick freely admitted was his
favourite—and as it was served with cream and sultanas
Isobel didn't object.

With the arrival of their coffee, Patrick fell unac-
countably silent, and Isobel wondered what he was thinking
as he stirred sugar into his cup. For her part, she knew she
would feel safer when she was securely back at the cottage.

She wanted to believe she could resist him, but she was afraid of what might happen if she was put to the test.

'Shall we go?'

'All right.'

Isobel nodded, and he left his chair to come and help her up. But she forestalled him, almost upsetting the coffee-pot in her haste to avoid his assistance, and then preceded him to the door.

Outside, it was dark now, and there were fewer people walking about. It enabled them to walk side by side without touching, though she was aware of Patrick's gaze when he looked her way.

'What are you doing next weekend?' he asked suddenly, and Isobel abandoned her uneasy introspection to give him a nervous look.

'Next weekend?' she echoed. 'Um—I'm not sure.'

Though, of course, she was, she reflected ruefully. She'd probably do the same as she'd done this weekend: a little shopping, a little cleaning, maybe even a little stocktaking. But without the added aggravation of taking her mother to Foxworth Hall.

'Would you like to be my guest at a party?' asked Patrick quietly. 'I shall be busy through the week, but I should be clear of any commitments by Saturday.'

Good for him!

Isobel felt impatient. What was he doing inviting her out again, almost as if they were any normal couple out on a date? He must know she'd only agreed to have dinner with him because he'd practically threatened her with eviction. And although she didn't seriously believe he would have gone through with it the fact remained that their relationship was artificial to say the least.

She took a deep breath. 'Well—thank you for inviting me, but—'

'But you're going to decline,' Patrick finished for her somewhat tersely. 'Why won't you accept my invitation? You've enjoyed yourself this evening, haven't you?' He sighed. 'I thought we were getting along together quite well.'

'That's as maybe—'

'But?'

'But I don't want to see you again.'

'Rubbish!'

'I beg your pardon?'

'I said that's rubbish,' he repeated irritably. Despite her efforts to avoid it, he took her arm to cross the road. 'I may have acted precipitately before—'

'Acted precipitately?' exclaimed Isobel heatedly. 'Is that how you describe it?'

'—but what happened was no violation,' he continued doggedly. 'We gave each other pleasure. What the hell is so wrong with that?'

'If you don't know—'

'I don't.'

Isobel gave him a disparaging look. 'I don't believe that. For heaven's sake—' She broke off as a group of young people briefly blocked their path, and then, when they were out of earshot, went on, 'You know you had no intention of seeing me again, until you saw me dining with Richard at your club.'

Patrick's jaw compressed. 'You don't know that.'

'Yes, I do.' The had reached the multi-storey car park now, and she stepped somewhat apprehensively into the lift that would take them to the sixth floor. Determined not to let him intimidate her, she looked up at him as the lift started its ascent. 'When did you decide to buy Foxworth Hall? I bet it was after we'd had that argument in the foyer!'

Patrick's eyes darkened. 'You think I bought Foxworth Hall because of you?'

Isobel realised how presumptuous that had sounded, and with burning cheeks she looked away. 'Does it matter?' she asked unsteadily. 'I'm not going to see you again. You can go ahead and threaten me all you like. I won't let you control my life.'

'Dammit, I'm not trying to control your life!' he exclaimed angrily. And then, almost unintentionally, it seemed, his hand cupped her throat, turning her face up to his.

Her eyes were wide with alarm and consternation as his mouth touched hers. He could not do this to her, she told herself. She was the mistress of her own destiny, and when this evening was over she would make sure she was never put in this position again. He was a brute, and an animal, for taking advantage of her. It was just her bad luck that they were alone in the lift.

But when she lifted her hands to push him away her senses betrayed her. When they encountered the warm silk that clothed his body, they spread and clung. Beneath her damp palms, she could feel the corded muscles of his belly, her nail snagging an opening, and finding the fine hair she remembered so well.

She tried to voice a protest, but it was no good. All that did was give him access to her mouth. And when his tongue slipped between her teeth to fill her with its hot strength she was reminded of how it had felt when he was a part of her, of that other heat pulsing between her legs.

'Oh, please . . .' she whispered weakly, her eyes closing, and Patrick sank back against the wall of the lift with her weight fully against him.

'You please me,' he said, cupping her face with his hands. His voice grew husky. 'More than anyone I've ever known.'

His hand slid behind her head and pressed her closer, angling her face so that the kiss deepened and lengthened, and drove all thoughts of resistance out of her mind. His arousal was taut against her stomach, and she couldn't prevent her hand from sliding down between them to cradle that throbbing hardness through the cloth.

'*God!*' he said hoarsely, and then the lift stopped and the doors slid back and allowed the cool air of reason to enter the cubicle. With a superhuman effort, Patrick propelled Isobel away from him, and she blinked somewhat disbelievingly as she stepped out onto the concrete floor.

It took Patrick a little longer to regain his equilibrium, but by the time they reached the car Isobel had recovered enough to notice what the wall of the lift had done to his clothes.

'Your suit's all dirty!' she exclaimed, reaching out automatically to brush his sleeve.

'To hell with the suit,' he answered shortly, taking off his jacket and flinging it onto the back seat. 'Get in,' he added, holding the door, and she got into the front without another word.

He didn't speak until they were out of town, and Isobel wasn't sure whether this was because he had to concentrate on his driving or to give himself time to think. She herself was grateful for the hiatus. Though she was no nearer to deciding what she ought to do when he did speak. It was easy to be firm when she wasn't with him, but when she was he had a disturbing way of confounding all her plans.

'I'm sorry,' he said, and for a moment she wondered if he was referring to the way he'd dismissed her concern about his suit. But his next words corrected this misapprehension. 'I'm not in the habit of—necking—in a lift.'

Isobel drew a breath. 'Nor am I,' she responded tautly, wondering if he was implying that she was.

But, 'I know that,' he said irritably. 'I'm not a complete moron. It's just—well, hell, you make me do things I can't justify.'

Isobel swallowed. 'What's that supposed to mean?'

'It means—' He cast a grim look in her direction. 'It means that you were right about my buying Foxworth Hall.' He paused, his eyes on the road, his features strained in the muted light from the dashboard. 'So don't tell me you can't see me again. We have to let this take its normal course.'

Isobel moistened her lips. 'I won't sleep with you again.'

Patrick gave an anguished laugh. 'Can you promise me that?'

'What do you mean?'

'Never mind.' He lifted one hand from the wheel as if in surrender. 'For the moment, I just want you to agree to come to the party next Saturday. I'll pick you up at half past six.' He hesitated. 'Will you do that?'

CHAPTER SEVENTEEN

ISOBEL had to answer the phone on Monday evening.

After a disturbed night, she'd left for the shop early on Monday morning, knowing her mother wouldn't try to get in touch with her there. Mrs Herriot knew of Chris's tendency to gossip as well as anyone, and she could never be sure that Isobel's young assistant wouldn't pick up the phone.

Besides, Isobel could always make the excuse of being busy at the shop, and there were always customers coming and going. What Mrs Herriot wanted to say was better said in private, and Isobel knew she couldn't avoid speaking to her mother for much longer.

So on Monday evening she felt obliged to pick up the receiver. She told herself it was because she owed her mother an explanation, but the truth was she was half afraid it might be Patrick trying to get in touch with her. After the reckless way he'd driven off the night before, she couldn't help being worried about him. Even though she'd agreed to go to the party with him, he'd still been in a curious mood when she'd left him.

Had he intended to spend the night at the cottage?

That was the question Isobel had asked herself as she'd got ready for bed. And what had he meant about her promising not to sleep with him? She didn't understand what was happening to her. She didn't understand *him*.

Her mother, conversely, was all too understandable. 'What is going on, Isobel?' she asked pre-emptively as soon as her daughter answered the phone. 'And where have you been? I rang this number at least a dozen times yesterday evening. I'm sure you were there. Your father said your car was parked at the gate when he was called out to old Mr Latimer.'

Isobel sighed, feeling the familiar nausea she had come to associate with this kind of conversation. 'I was out, Mum,' she insisted. And then, deciding there was no point in avoiding the issue, she added, 'I had dinner with—with Patrick Shannon.'

'With Patrick Shannon?' Mrs Herriot didn't sound so much disbelieving as shocked. 'Well...' She took a moment to gather her composure, before continuing tersely, 'You might have told me you were friends before we went to Foxworth Hall.'

Isobel sighed. 'I—why—we're not exactly friends,' she mumbled unwillingly, aware that she was digging a pit for herself but unable to allow her mother to assume that she'd been deceiving her all along. 'I—we—last night was the first time he's taken me out.'

Isobel grimaced. Well, it was true, she consoled herself defensively, realising there was no way she could tell her mother anything else. Just imagining describing their real relationship brought her out in a sweat. Mrs Herriot might want her daughter to get married, but she'd draw the line at her sleeping with a man she barely knew.

'I'm afraid I don't understand,' declared her mother at last. 'How did you meet this man? And what can he possibly want with you? I wouldn't have thought you were the kind of woman he'd find attractive. Unless he thinks that because you're inexperienced you're vulnerable.'

Isobel tried not to feel hurt, but her mother's words stung just the same. The trouble was, they mirrored her own anxieties about the relationship, and the way Patrick had behaved last night hadn't helped.

'I met him when he came into the shop,' she replied, managing, not without some effort, to keep her tone neutral. 'As for what he sees in me, Mum, not all men are looking for surface gloss. Perhaps he finds me intelligent. Stranger things have happened.'

Mrs Herriot seemed to realise she had been less than complimentary, and hurried to make amends. 'Well, of course, dear,' she said. 'I'm not implying that you're *not* attractive. It's just that—well, in that article I mentioned

he was photographed with a rather attractive *older* woman.
And my impression of him was that he played his cards
very close to his chest.'

'Because he wouldn't discuss our association with you?'
asked Isobel shrewdly, and her mother took a sudden intake
of breath.

'I think that was uncalled for, Isobel,' she retorted. 'But
you must know a man like him wants only one thing.'

Isobel wanted to laugh and cry in equal measures.
'Honestly, Mum!' she exclaimed. 'Where have you been?
If you're talking about sex, then say so. And I doubt if
Patrick Shannon goes short of that.'

'Well, really!' Mrs Herriot didn't like this turn in the
conversation. 'I must say I never expected a daughter of
mine to be so coarse. But mark my words, that man has a
hidden agenda. You may think his designs are innocent,
but I know better.'

That you do, Mum, thought Isobel wryly, wishing she
could just hang up. Her mother's words had resurrected all
her own misgivings, and she was already wishing she'd been
firmer the night before.

'So when are you seeing him again?' asked Mrs Herriot.
'I assume you are seeing him, as you're defending him so
passionately.'

'I am not defending him passionately!'

'But you are seeing him again?'

'All right. Yes. He's taking me to a party on Saturday
night.' Isobel's nails dug into her palms. 'I thought you'd
be delighted to hear I'm having a social life at last.'

'With a man like that!'

Mrs Herriot's tone was eloquent of her disapproval, and
Isobel felt a twinge of pique. 'What's wrong with him,
Mum? He's older than I am, he's certainly eligible, and
he's not married. What more do I want, for heaven's sake?'

'You're not implying that Patrick Shannon might ask you
to marry him?'

Mrs Herriot couldn't hide her scepticism now, and Isobel
could hardly speak for the constriction in her throat. 'Of
course not,' she said, not caring what her mother thought

now, only needing to expunge some of her own bitterness. 'He wants to go to bed with me, just like you said!'

It was a depressing week.

From being unusually dry, the weather turned to rain, and Isobel's customers declined accordingly. No one wanted to trudge about Horsham in the pouring rain. The bus tours, which weeks before had used Horsham as a convenient stopping-off point, now drove on to Oxford or Stratford, where there were covered malls to walk in.

In addition to which, Isobel wished that whatever was wrong with her would go away. She was fed up with feeling under the weather, fed up with the suspicion that Patrick Shannon was to blame.

Her mother's cast was removed on Wednesday, and she made Isobel's cottage her first port of call. Isobel had hoped she'd have too much to do picking up the threads of her business, but she had an able assistant who had borne the burden while she was incapacitated, and she was apparently in no hurry to return and take control.

Even so, her visit was brief and, from her point of view, unsatisfactory. After a couple of days spent filling in time at her own shop, Isobel was in no mood to be sociable. Even her mother's efforts to assure her that she had meant nothing disparaging in her comments about Patrick Shannon fell on stony ground. She departed with a rather wounded air that Isobel knew she would have to repair before too long.

And as the week wore on she began to wish she had never accepted Patrick's invitation. It was causing her far too much soul-searching, and without his disturbing presence to influence her she was finding it harder and harder to understand why she'd let him persuade her. Her mother was right. Any interest Patrick Shannon had in her was purely transient. She was getting worked up—and alienating her family—for no good reason that she could see.

But without resorting to dubious methods there was no way she could get in touch with him to call it off. She knew his private number would be unlisted, and the idea of ringing

Shannon Holdings and leaving a message seemed too impersonal.

Which was why she decided to buy herself a new outfit on Friday. If she was obliged to attend this party, then the least she could do was ensure she looked respectable, she told herself firmly. It was nothing to do with what her mother had said, nor a puerile attempt to win Patrick's admiration.

In consequence, she closed the shop early on Friday afternoon and drove the fifteen miles to Stratford in the little Peugeot. Parking where she had parked with Patrick, she determinedly used the stairs instead of the lift. She didn't need reminding of what had happened last Sunday evening. She didn't want to anticipate what *might* happen on Saturday night.

She found what she was looking for in a small boutique just off the high street. It was not the sort of shop she would normally have patronised, catering as it did for a much younger clientele. But she was pleasantly surprised to find many more mature styles among the spandex vests and leather miniskirts, and the customers weren't all skinny teenagers.

It eventually came down to a choice between two outfits: one was a cream silk ribbed dress with a round neckline, no sleeves and a short skirt, and the other was a calf-length wraparound sheath, made of black silk jersey and edged with white.

Both dresses looked good, she had to admit, but although she would have liked to choose the minidress it didn't have half the elegance of the silk jersey. Besides, although she chided her lack of courage, the black dress was more her style.

She thought of having her hair cut and styled too as she passed a beauty salon, but she drew the line at changing her appearance. A new dress was called for; a make-over wasn't. She'd hate her mother to think she was trying to compete with the women Patrick was used to.

Nonetheless, she did spend some time coiling her hair into a loose knot on Saturday evening. It took what seemed like a hundred hairpins to achieve the effect she was seeking, but she was satisfied that it looked secure as well as casual when the last pin had been inserted.

She took more time over her make-up, too, using a cream foundation and accentuating her eyes with a dark eyeliner. Her lashes were long, and only needed a touch of mascara at the tips, while a subtle amber lipstick gave definition to her mouth.

She put the dress on last, taking care not to smudge her make-up, or mark the pristine piping that bordered every hem. Its wraparound style was complimentary to the fullness of her breasts, but she wore a seamless bra to try and disguise their wilful display.

Opaque tights hid all but the shape of her ankles, and high-heeled strappy shoes added inches to her height. Twirling before her mirror, she knew a foolish sense of excitement. She had never looked so sophisticated before.

The doorbell rang as she was adding a comb to her purse, and the breath caught in her throat. Did she really look all right? she wondered. Or was her opinion hopelessly naïve? Could her dress really compete with clothes from Jasper Conran or Donna Karan? And they were just what was available in London. Patrick Shannon's sister probably bought her clothes in Paris.

Deciding it was too late to worry about that now, she grimaced at her reflection, and then went slowly downstairs. She told herself she couldn't hurry, because she didn't want to run the risk of spoiling her hair. But the truth was, she was putting off the moment when Patrick would see her. She was so afraid he wouldn't be impressed.

Her hand trembled as she reached for the latch, but, controlling her nerves, she opened the door wide. The words 'I'm ready,' froze on her lips. It wasn't Patrick. It was the chauffeur, Joe, who stood waiting outside.

'Hello,' he said. 'I'm Joe Muzambe.'

'I know who you are.' Isobel knew a momentary pang of nausea. 'Isn't P—your employer—here?'

'He sent me to pick you up,' explained Joe ruefully. 'I hope you don't mind. He had a last-minute meeting to attend.'

Isobel's doubts reasserted themselves. 'A last-minute meeting?' she echoed. 'Where?'

'Oh, at Company House,' said Joe dismissively, gesturing towards the Bentley, which was waiting at the gate. 'I don't want to rush you, but I am running a couple of minutes late.'

Isobel still hesitated. She wanted to ask what kind of meeting took place at six-thirty on a Saturday evening. She wanted to know where this party was being held, and where they were expected to meet. But Joe had already reached the gate, and it seemed churlish to delay him. Why hadn't Patrick phoned and explained that he couldn't pick her up himself?

Irritation with herself—and Patrick—set in, and although she wasn't at all happy about these new arrangements she didn't see that she had a lot of choice but to fall in with them. She could phone Patrick, she supposed. Joe was bound to know his number. But how could she justify bringing him out of his meeting? If she'd been more experienced in these matters, she might have had more confidence. As it was, she simply locked the door and followed Joe down the path.

She hadn't been in the back of the Bentley before. She would have preferred to sit in the front, but Joe was holding the rear door open when she reached the car, and it occurred to her that they were probably going to pick Patrick up too. That idea was reassuring, until she remembered where Joe had said the meeting was taking place, and, feeling a headache probing at her temples, Isobel gave up trying to second-guess him.

Joe put on some music, and the mellow strains of a Debussy étude dispelled her foolish fears. What did it matter whether Joe or Patrick drove her to the party? She wasn't in any hurry to see Patrick. And at least she wasn't obliged to make small talk with Joe.

She was tired, and the car was wonderfully comfortable. It became an effort to keep her eyes open, and eventually she let them close. Her head tipped back against the leather upholstery, and she felt a sense of well-being envelop her. She would just relax for a few minutes, and then she'd ask Joe where he was taking her.

It was the vibration of the other traffic that awakened her. That, and the constant obstructions of driving in London. She knew it was London, because she recognised the buses. Even Oxford wasn't as busy as this—not even in the rush hour.

She blinked, trying to get her bearings, and then leaned forward to touch Joe on the shoulder. 'Where are we?' she asked, alarmed at the thought of how long she had slept, and how trusting she had been.

'Knightsbridge,' replied Joe laconically, braking to allow one of the buses that had alerted her to her whereabouts to pull away. 'We'll be there in a few minutes.' His eyes crinkled in the rear-view mirror. 'Did the music put you to sleep?'

Isobel took a deep breath. 'Where will we be in a few minutes?' she demanded. 'Where is this—party being held?'

'Don't you know?' Joe saw her expression and hastily explained, 'Why, it's at Pat's house in Lauriston Square. I thought you knew.'

CHAPTER EIGHTEEN

ISOBEL'S jaw sagged. 'His *house*?' she echoed faintly.

'That's right.' His eyes narrowed assessingly. 'You didn't know.'

Isobel shook her head. 'I thought—oh, I suppose I thought it was going to be somewhere near Horsham.' She realised now how foolish that sounded. She swallowed, and then stiffened. 'Will you be taking me home?'

Joe shrugged. 'If that's what you want.'

'It is.' Isobel was very sure about that. Once again, Patrick had tricked her, and she had no intention of staying at his house.

She was wondering if he'd tricked her in another way, too. Was there really a party at all, or was this his way of getting her alone? A couple of hours ago that prospect would not have been so bleak, but now she was in a turmoil of indignation.

Her doubts about the former were quickly answered. When they turned from Windsor Court into Lauriston Square, it was almost impossible to find anywhere to park. Every kind of expensive car, including a few Ferraris and a Maserati, was double-banked in places, with the little railed garden in the centre of the square completely over-shadowed by their bulk.

Daylight was beginning to fade, too, and a quick look at her watch informed her that it was after eight o'clock. Dear God, was she to be the last to arrive? Would she be forced to make an entrance? She hoped Patrick wouldn't desert her. She wasn't used to social occasions like this.

Joe was forced to double-park too, and because she was shaking so much he was out of the car and round to open the door for her before she could gather her wits. 'Take it easy,' he said gently, as if sensing her indecision. 'Pat's not so bad, believe me! He's been a good friend to me.'

Isobel gave him a rueful look. 'Is it so obvious?'

'That you're apprehensive?' He grinned. 'Just a little. But don't you let it spoil your evening. He's giving this party for you.'

'For me?'

Isobel's throat felt tight, and Joe helped her out onto the pavement. 'Sure. He's not a party animal, whatever you may have read about him.'

'So, why—?'

But she never got to finish her sentence. Behind her, the door to the tall, elegant town house had opened, and a flood of light came down the steps and caught them in its warm, encircling glow. And, blocking the light as he came, Patrick ran down the steps to join them, his eyes meeting Isobel's and answering all her questions at once.

'I thought you were never going to get here,' he said, his arm slipping about her waist as if it were the most natural thing in the world.

'You didn't allow for the traffic,' said Joe, slamming the rear door. 'And you forgot to tell the lady that I'd be bringing her back to town.'

Patrick's mouth twisted with a mixture of impatience and humour, but his eyes were rueful as he turned to Isobel. 'I was afraid you wouldn't come,' he admitted, apparently uncaring that Joe was present. 'Never mind. You're here now. And I'm hoping you're going to enjoy yourself.'

Joe touched Isobel's sleeve. 'What time would you like to leave?' he asked, and for the first time Patrick's expression showed some irritation.

'Don't worry about Isobel,' he said. 'We'll make our own arrangements. You can take the car if you like. I'm sure Lucille will find it more comfortable than your old heap.'

Isobel hesitated. 'I did ask—Joe—if he would—'

'Forget it.' Patrick was doing his best to hide his anger. 'Come on.' He urged her up the steps. 'Let's go and get a drink.'

Isobel cast a helpless look over her shoulder as she accompanied Patrick up the steps, and Joe lifted his hand in a gesture of farewell. But as they reached the well-lit entrance Isobel felt a momentary return of anxiety, and she wished she'd been more decisive, instead of just giving in.

Still, if she wanted to go home—*when* she wanted to go home—she could always call a taxi to take her to the station, she told herself reassuringly, gazing somewhat bemusedly about her as Patrick closed the door. They were standing in the foyer, a glittering chandelier above their heads providing the illumination, and she had never seen anything more elegant in her life.

'You look beautiful,' said Patrick huskily, making no effort to release her, and Isobel was suddenly glad he'd sent Joe away. It was pointless to pretend she wasn't attracted to this man, and the idea of being here, in his house, had a potency all its own.

'Do I?' she asked, and he bent his head and brushed the nape of her neck with his tongue.

'Is this all for me?' he murmured against her skin. 'God, I wish we were here alone.'

So did she, but she didn't say so, and having been reminded that they were not alone in the house, she looked somewhat apprehensively about her. 'Your guests,' she ventured unevenly, finding it difficult to speak. 'Won't they be wondering where you are?'

'Probably,' he conceded whimsically, glancing at the ceiling, and she became aware of the buzz of sound above their heads. 'Come on,' he said. 'They're waiting to meet you. I'm sorry if it sounds like an ordeal. But if it's any consolation I'll be with you.' His eyes darkened. 'All night.'

They mounted a staircase with delicately carved spindles which were polished to a high shine. It swept up from the foyer, following the contours of a carpeted hall which disappeared towards the back of the house. The stairs were carpeted too, and Isobel's feet sank into the luxurious pile. One of her friends at college had lived in a house like this, with the drawing room on the first floor and the bedrooms on the floor above. But it hadn't been in Knightsbridge, and it hadn't been decorated with such style. Isobel had never seen such a fabulous house before.

The room they entered, through double panelled doors, appeared to stretch from the front to the back of the house, and Isobel's first impression was that it was full of people. Patrick's guests—and there were many—were all talking and laughing and enjoying drinks before partaking of the buffet supper that was laid out at one end of the room. A hi-fi added its own melodic contribution, but the overall sense was one of noise.

Isobel had hoped they might slip into the room unobserved, but she should have known that that would be too good to be true. However, the group of people who were standing nearest the door, and who saw them at once, absorbed them into their number, and although she was vaguely apprehensive no one questioned who she was.

Someone thrust a glass of what she later realised was champagne into her hand, and she found it was fairly easy to join in the conversation. There were no formal introductions, as she had feared, and Patrick's friends accepted her presence without hesitation.

The only personal question she was asked came when one of the women showed admiration for the silver coils she had threaded through her ears. Or course, when she told her they'd been made by an elderly man who supplied costume jewellery for the craft shop, she received a few more queries about what she sold. But these people weren't really interested in her small enterprise—not when most of the jewellery she had seen was worth more than what the craft shop earned in a year.

If they were curious about her, they had been warned not to show it. And Patrick was making no secret of the fact that she was his guest. If he had to leave her alone, he always made sure someone else was looking after her while he was gone. If she hadn't known better, she'd have suspected he was trying to prove a point.

She wondered what his friends really thought of her. What conclusions had they drawn about how—and why—she was here? Did they think she was just an aberration? Or a novelty he'd tire of before long?

They were reasonable assumptions. Looking round the luxurious room, with its silk-clad walls and velvet curtains, its crystal chandeliers and soft leather sofas, she reminded herself that she should not take anything he said seriously.

He wanted her; that much she accepted. Why else had he brought her all this way? But her mother was right: he wasn't going to marry her. Why should he? What she offered was hardly unique.

A shiver ran down her spine, and suddenly she wished she hadn't accepted his invitation. She didn't like the idea that these people regarded her as Patrick's current toy. It didn't matter if half the women present probably occupied a similar position with their partners. She had always considered herself immune to casual sex.

'Are you OK?'

As if he'd sensed her uncertainty, Patrick was suddenly beside her, twisting an errant strand of her hair around his finger, allowing the pad of his thumb to brush her neck. He was wearing a dark suit this evening, and Isobel thought he had never looked more attractive. She knew a crazy need to put her brand upon him.

'Do it,' he murmured, his eyes searching her face and finding the emotion she was trying so hard to hide. 'Kiss me,' he said, apparently uncaring of the other conversations that were going on around him, and, bending his head, he dipped his tongue into her mouth.

Isobel's senses swam. 'Don't,' she protested, when she could get her breath, but she could see the mocking scepticism in his eyes. He knew exactly what he was doing, she thought, and she was foolish enough to let him.

'All right.' His knuckle caressed her cheek as he drew his hand away, and she felt the fiery heat that rose inside her at his careless touch. 'We've got plenty of time,' he added, rescuing two more glasses of champagne from the tray carried by a passing waiter. 'What do you think of the party? Are you enjoying yourself?'

Isobel took the glass he offered, grateful for the barrier it presented. 'It's—interesting,' she said. And then, more honestly, she asked, 'Do you know all these people? There must be fifty guests in this room.'

'Nearer eighty, actually,' admitted Patrick drily. 'And no, I don't know all of them in truth. They're business colleagues, mostly, whose wives I suppose I should know but don't.'

Isobel glanced around. 'Do you give many parties?'

'No.'

His answer was surprisingly terse, and she frowned. 'I thought you would.'

'Because it goes with the image you have of me?' he suggested. 'It may surprise you, but I don't live a very exciting life. I enjoy my work and I enjoy my leisure. But it doesn't usually include entertaining guests at home.'

'What do you mean?'

'I mean I usually entertain guests at clubs or restaurants. This is an exception. At the risk of sounding conceited, I'd say that's why half these people are here.'

Isobel blinked. 'Because they haven't been here before?'

'Because they haven't been here before,' he agreed evenly. 'Come along. Let me get you something to eat.'

Isobel followed him, but she was still curious. 'You haven't lived here long?' she asked, and Patrick gave her a wry look.

'I've lived here six years,' he said. 'Ever since my— divorce. My ex-wife commandeered the family home.'

Isobel stared at him and Patrick's brows drew together. 'I wasn't the guilty party, if that's what you're thinking. I let Amanda have the house to get her off my back.'

Isobel still looked doubtful, and Patrick expelled an impatient sigh. 'It's the truth, dammit,' he muttered. 'Ask anyone who knows me.'

Isobel moistened her lips. 'Do you—I mean—are there— children?'

'No.' His lips thinned. 'Thank God!'

'What do you mean?'

'Well, I can imagine the mileage Amanda would have got out of the poor brats if there were. My ex-wife was—is— a greedy woman, Belle. If there'd been children to fight over, she'd have got my trousers as well as the shirt off my back.'

Isobel permitted herself to look up at him. 'You're exaggerating.'

'Am I? You don't know her like I do.'

'But—you must have loved her once.' Isobel caught her lip between her teeth. 'You married her.'

'What's love got to do with marriage?' enquired Patrick grimly, spooning some caviare onto a cracker and popping it into her mouth. The food kept her silent but, anyway, she didn't have an answer for him. And his words had only confirmed something she already knew.

She'd tasted caviare before, had quite liked it in fact, but tonight it didn't agree with her. It took an enormous effort to get the salty substance down her throat, and even then she felt her stomach heave.

'Um—where's the bathroom?' she asked, setting down her glass, and Patrick regarded her pale face with some concern.

'I'm sorry,' he said. 'I'm afraid I just assumed you'd like it.' And then, realising he was wasting time, he added, 'Follow me.'

It was cooler on the landing outside, and a little of Isobel's nausea subsided. But she was grateful when he showed her into a spacious bathroom, and, locking the door, she hurried to the sink.

Five minutes later, Patrick tapped on the door.

Isobel was sitting exhaustedly on the cream leather-topped stool that faced the mirrored vanity and, looking at her drawn face, she wished she didn't have to open the door. Her eyes looked huge, and her mouth had lost all trace of lipstick. She would have to make some repairs before he saw her again.

'Belle!' His voice was insistent. 'Belle, open the door, for God's sake. Are you all right?'

'I'm—fine,' she said faintly, clearly sounding as if she wasn't. 'Just give me a few minutes to tidy my hair.'

'Open the door,' he persisted. 'I want to see for myself that you're all right. Look—' he was keeping his temper in check with obvious difficulty '—this is my goddamned bathroom! Don't force me to break the door.'

Isobel drew a painful breath and, leaning forward, ran her fingers under the cold-water tap and quickly cleaned her teeth. It was his bathroom, she acknowledged, and she had no wish to draw attention to herself by causing a scene. But when she went to the door and opened it her face mirrored the indignation she was feeling.

Patrick cast one look at her and then bundled her back into the room. He looked about him, as if seeking some secret she wasn't telling him, and then cupped her hot face in his cool hands. 'Poor Belle,' he crooned, his thumbs stroking the dark shadows that had appeared beneath her eyes. 'Would you like me to get rid of all these people so that we can go to bed?'

Isobel caught her breath. 'No!'

'You're feeling better?'

'Whether I'm feeling better or not has nothing to do with it. I mean—I'm not going to bed with you,' said Isobel unsteadily, knocking his hands away. 'In fact I think I'd like to leave. I am feeling a bit—dizzy. Perhaps you'd make my apologies and—'

'All right. I'll come with you,' said Patrick at once, and Isobel gave him a disbelieving look.

'You can't.'

'Why can't I?'

Isobel licked her lips. 'You've been drinking.'

'Two glasses of champagne does not make me a danger to anyone else.'

That was a matter of opinion.

'Nevertheless—'

'OK. We'll take a cab.' Patrick's jaw compressed warningly. 'Just don't expect me to let you go on your own.'

Isobel shook her head. 'You have guests...'

'I'll explain.'

'Oh, yes?' Isobel cringed at the thought of his explanation. 'Pat, please; you're embarrassing me. Can't you see that? I—I want to go on my own.'

'Why?'

Isobel sighed. 'Because—because I need to think.'

'What about?'

His marriage, his attitude towards love—everything...

'Things,' she said at last, turning away from him and examining her reflection in the mirror. 'Oh, God, I look a mess,' she groaned, forgetting for a moment that he could hear her, and Patrick put his arms around her from behind.

'You don't look a mess,' he assured her thickly, his hands shaping the slight swell of her abdomen, before moving up to cup the rounded fullness of her breasts. He pressed her back against him, and she could feel the muscled hardness of his body. 'Let me come with you, or stay here,' he begged, and she quivered. 'I love you, Belle. I mean it. And you're driving me crazy!'

'*Patrick!*'

The female voice was unfamiliar. Isobel, who had closed her eyes against the raw temptation of his words, opened them again to find a strange woman staring angrily at them from the doorway. She was tall and slim and dark, so it wasn't Joanna. But there was something familiar about her, and whoever she was she caused Patrick to let her go.

'Jillian,' he said, and even through her own sense of outrage Isobel heard the weary frustration in his voice. 'I'd given you up an hour ago.' So he had invited his sister! 'What was the delay? Did Richard prick his finger?'

Richard!

'No, I'm here.' A man appeared beside the woman and put a possessive arm about her waist. He was looking at Jillian as he spoke, so he didn't immediately notice Patrick's companion. He nuzzled her neck. 'You're not the only one who likes to play.'

'Anyway, aren't you going to introduce us to your lady-friend?' Jillian demanded, clearly in no mood to suffer her husband's teasing. 'That is why you invited us here, isn't it? Though I have to say I don't think much of your choice of venue.'

Isobel's humiliation was complete. Patrick had invited his sister here to meet her, knowing full well how she would react to Isobel's presence. Not to mention her husband. Her lips curled at the thought of how Richard had attempted to break his vows.

She must have made some sound, either of pain or of mortification, because Richard looked up. And it was almost worth it to see how her appearance affected him.

'My God—I-*Isobel*!' he stuttered, her name setting light to the situation. 'Pat, what—what the hell's going on?' The sweat stood out on his forehead. 'Is this some kind of joke?'

'*Isobel?*'

Jillian said the word now, and Isobel looked at Patrick with pain-filled eyes. 'How could you?' she cried. 'How could you do this?' She pressed a hand to her throat. 'You're sick!'

'You don't understand, Belle—'

'Belle?' repeated Richard stupidly. 'What's going on here? Are you saying you and Isobel—?'

'Are an item?' finished his wife coldly. 'I hardly think so, do you?' She sneered. 'No, this is Pat's little way of undermining our relationship—bringing this little tart here and exposing your guilt!'

'Jill—'

'It isn't like that,' said Patrick harshly, trying to get hold of Isobel's arm, but she evaded him. 'For God's sake, all of you, listen to me. I brought Belle here because I care about her—'

'Oh, please!' Patently, Jillian didn't believe him, and Isobel couldn't blame her. 'You're saying that this woman means something to you?'

'Yes—'

'No!' Jillian's eyes glittered, and the look she cast at Isobel was disparaging. 'You brought her here to embarrass all of us, and you succeeded.'

'Jillian—'

'What? *What?*' She gazed at him with almost as much contempt as she'd saved for Isobel. 'You'll be telling us next that you've asked her to marry you.' Her brows arched. 'Or perhaps that's too much of a gamble, even for you.'

Patrick's jaw clamped, and Isobel, whose eyes had been drawn to him by his sister's accusation, felt something inside her collapse and die. She could see it in his face: marrying her had never been an option. The triumph in Jillian's eyes was the last thing she saw as she pushed her way out of the room.

CHAPTER NINETEEN

'MISS HERRIOT?'

The woman standing at the other side of the counter had addressed her politely, but Isobel gave her a wary look. She'd come into the shop a few moments ago, and, although she'd appeared to be examining the merchandise, as soon as the last customer had departed she'd come straight across to speak to her.

She wasn't Isobel's usual type of customer. For one thing, the suit she was wearing was obviously Chanel, and her carefully coiffed curls had not been styled by an amateur hand. Her hair was tinted, to make the most of her youthful appearance, but Isobel guessed she had to be at least fifty, or perhaps sixty was nearer the mark.

'Yes?' she said, and her tone was decidedly crisp, but she couldn't help it. The news she had had a few days ago was still giving her sleepless nights, and if, as she suspected, this woman had brought a message from Patrick she didn't want to know.

'I thought it must be,' declared the woman, her smile as restrained as her appearance. 'How do you do? I'm Susannah Riker-Shannon.' She paused. 'I believe you know my son.'

Riker-Shannon?

Isobel swallowed, the urge to be rude escaping her for the moment. 'Mrs—Riker-Shannon,' she said stiffly. 'Yes. How do you do?' She moistened her dry lips. 'Patrick shouldn't have sent you here.'

'He didn't.' Susannah Riker-Shannon glanced ruefully about her. 'In fact, he'd be furious if he knew.' She sighed. 'But someone had to do something.' She turned back, and now her smile was a trifle forced. 'He's so like his father— my late husband.'

'Really?'

172

Isobel told herself she didn't want to hear this. Just because the messenger was different, it didn't make the message any more important to her. She didn't want to see Patrick. She'd told him that already. She didn't even want to speak to him. As far as she was concerned, she *never* wanted to see him again.

Despite the fact that—she wrapped her arms protectively about herself—she might *have* to...

'Yes, really,' declared Patrick's mother, her expression losing its cordial appearance. She looked towards the door. 'Could you possibly close the shop? I'd prefer us not to be disturbed.'

Isobel's lips parted. The arrogance of these people amazed her. 'I'm afraid that is out of the question,' she found pleasure in saying. 'I have my living to earn, Mrs Riker-Shannon. And it is one of the busiest times of the day.'

'It doesn't look it.' Susannah Riker-Shannon surveyed the empty shop with some asperity. 'I'm serious, Miss Herriot. I need to speak to you. I think you owe it to Patrick to hear what I have to say.'

Isobel gasped. 'I don't *owe* Patrick anything.'

'Don't you?' His mother looked pointedly at her, and just for a moment Isobel wondered if she could see the secret she was hiding in her face. But then she went on, 'You've judged him without being prepared to listen to his explanation. At least have the decency to let me give you that.'

'To what end?' Isobel felt a tremor of apprehension sweep over her, but she dismissed it. 'Your son used me, Mrs Riker-Shannon. And then humiliated me in front of his family and friends.'

'He knows he hurt you—'

'Oh, thanks.'

'—but you have to understand it wasn't intended to be that way.'

'I don't see what other way it could have been.'

'No. I see that. But if you'd give me a few moments of your time I'd like to explain.'

Isobel sighed, weariness enveloping her. 'There's nothing to explain, Mrs Riker-Shannon.'

'Oh, for heaven's sake, call me Susannah. Or Susie, if you will.' Her eyes drifted for a moment. 'Patrick—my husband Patrick, that is—used to call me Susie. But then he died, and my granddaughter inherited the name.'

Isobel's lips felt tight. 'Really, Mrs— I'm sure you mean well by coming here, but—'

'But you're not prepared to give me a few minutes of your time.' The woman's face mirrored her frustration. 'Don't you care about my son at all?'

Isobel stiffened. 'I think you'd better go.'

'Why? Because I've asked you a question you can't dismiss as easily as you've dismissed the rest?'

'It's not a question of dismissing anything.' Isobel gave a resigned sigh, and then gave in. 'What is it you want, Mrs Riker-Shannon? I can't believe you care what happens to me, any more than your daughter does.'

'Jillian!' Patrick's mother dismissed her daughter with an impatient snort. 'I suggest you ignore anything Jillian said, and put it down to good, old-fashioned jealousy. She thought you had been having an affair with her husband, Miss Herriot. And no one had chosen to tell her that it wasn't true.'

Isobel held up her head. 'Oh, I realise that.'

'Do you?' The older woman regarded her steadily. 'Then do you also realise that Patrick's intention in inviting you to a party he'd engineered for your benefit was to give his sister a chance to meet you face to face?'

Isobel stared. 'I do now. It happened, Mrs Riker-Shannon. We met face to face all right. Didn't your daughter tell you that?'

Patrick's mother sighed. 'You're jumping to conclusions again,' she said quietly. 'My son knows his sister—considerably better than you do, I suggest. He knew she'd never agree to meet you voluntarily. But in a room full of people he gambled that she wouldn't make a scene.'

Isobel shook her head. 'But why would he want us to meet? To prove to Jillian that her husband wasn't having an affair?'

'No!' The older woman was impatient. 'I'd hazard a guess that if Jillian and Richard did split up he'd be very pleased.'

'Then—'

'He wanted Jillian to meet you because he cares about you!' exclaimed his mother distractedly. 'My son's in love with you, Miss Herriot, and I can't allow the situation to go on.'

'What situation?' Isobel blinked.

'This situation,' declared the woman tersely. 'Your refusing to speak to him, to go and see him, and Patrick not caring if the company survives or fails.'

Isobel made a choked sound. 'Aren't you exaggerating? Just a tiny bit? I can't believe that the future of Shannon Holdings is dependent on whether I see Patrick or not.'

'No?' The other woman regarded her with eyes that were suspiciously bright suddenly. 'Well, take my word for it, Patrick is the force behind Shannon Holdings. If there was any suspicion that he couldn't continue—'

'But why should there be?' Isobel stared back, a twinge of what she refused to recognise as panic clutching her insides. 'You're not telling me Patrick's—ill?' Her lips twisted. 'He seemed disgustingly healthy a couple of weeks ago.'

Patrick's mother sniffed. 'Well, he was—' She broke off. 'But now he's not.'

Isobel felt the clutching hand tighten. 'What's wrong with him?'

'Does that matter?' The woman gave a helpless shrug. 'You apparently won't even speak to him on the phone.'

Isobel was silent. She could have said that of course it mattered, that even hearing that he wasn't well drove a knife through her heart. But she suspected that that was what she was supposed to say. Despite the woman's apparent sincerity, how could she trust her?

'I'm sorry,' she said at last. 'I'm sorry if he's not well, and in spite of everything I hope he soon gets better. But I can't help you, Mrs Riker-Shannon. I—whatever there was between—between your son and me is over.'

'But he loves you!'

'Does he?'

'Yes.' The woman licked her lips and then her shoulders sagged. 'Oh, God, I said I wouldn't tell you, but I've got to. He was shot, Miss Herriot. Patrick was shot!'

Isobel swayed. 'Shot?' She felt sick. 'I—who—?'

'It was a man called Conrad Martin. He escaped from prison ten days ago, and because Patrick hasn't been taking the usual precautions recently this man was waiting for him when he went down to the garage to collect his car.'

'But aren't there guards—security people—?'

'Yes, usually. But if someone is determined enough they'll find a way.'

'And—and is he badly hurt?'

'Fortunately, no. As luck would have it, one of the concrete pillars took most of the blast, and he only got the deflection. There's always the danger of infection with gunshot wounds, but so long as he takes his medication he should be all right.'

'Oh, God!' Isobel felt suddenly weak, and she gripped the edge of the counter with both hands. 'But why didn't he tell me?' She frowned, still suspicious. 'Why hasn't there been anything in the Press?'

'Luckily, we've managed to keep it out of the newspapers. To avoid a run on the company's shares, if nothing else. You know what the market's like; any hint of trouble and people get worried. But unless Patrick pulls himself together it won't matter either way.'

Isobel was sweating. She could feel the perspiration trickling down her spine, and although it wasn't a particularly warm day there didn't seem to be any air. Patrick had been shot; he could have been killed, and she would have known nothing about it. Was that really what she wanted? Was her pride worth more than Patrick's life?

'The other man,' she ventured, to give herself time to think. 'What—what happened to him?'

'Martin?' Mrs Riker-Shannon gave a shudder. 'Thankfully, he's back in prison. A psychiatric unit this time. The man's obviously mentally disturbed.'

Isobel made a helpless gesture. 'Where is he?'

'Who? Martin?'

'No.'

Isobel was finding it difficult to speak, and Patrick's mother seemed to realise that the younger woman was suffering from shock. 'Believe it or not, he insists on staying at Foxworth. That's why I'm so worried. Patrick never was much good at looking after himself.'

Isobel had seen Joe once since the night he'd driven her home from London.

On that occasion he'd been sitting outside the shop in the car, waiting for Patrick, but as Isobel had refused to speak to his employer she hadn't had a chance to thank Joe again for being there when she'd needed him. And he had been there for her, when Isobel had rushed out into Lauriston Square on that awful evening. Far from taking Patrick's advice, and taking his lady out for the evening, he'd waited to assure himself that Isobel didn't need him. And she'd been so grateful that he had.

Which was why she wasn't surprised that it was Joe who came out to meet her when she parked the little Peugeot outside Foxworth Hall. It wouldn't have occurred to Joe Muzambe not to stay with his employer, even if the circumstances he was having to live under were vastly different from what he was used to.

'Hey,' he said as she got not altogether steadily out of the car. 'How are you? Thanks for coming.'

Isobel gazed at him. 'You *knew* I was coming?' she asked, suspicion rearing its ugly head again, and Joe gave her a rueful look.

'I hoped,' he said honestly. 'I knew Pat's mother was going to see you. Did she tell you what happened? Did she tell you he nearly got himself killed?'

Isobel let her breath out on a long sigh. 'So it's true, then?'

'That Pat was shot? You better believe it. That guy Martin's had it in for him for years, ever since the council moved his caravan off some land that Shannon Holdings intended to develop. It didn't matter that Pat found him an alternative site; the man just hated authority. He threatened Pat once before and this time he made it.'

Isobel shuddered. 'I had no idea.'

'No.' Joe closed the door of her car for her, and gestured towards the house. 'Well, I guess you want to see him. He's in the orangery. It's not very comfortable, but it's better than the rest of the house.'

Isobel moistened her lips. 'Does he—does Patrick know his mother came to see me?'

Joe shrugged. 'He didn't hear it from me.'

Which wasn't quite an answer, but Isobel couldn't wait any longer. She was already regretting the impulse that had brought her here, and she knew that if she delayed she'd chicken out.

The atmosphere struck her as chill when they entered the vaulted hall, and with the coolness of evening enveloping its thick walls the house felt like a tomb.

But that was too fanciful, she told herself. Patrick had been shot, but he wasn't dying, and she was only here because his mother had aroused her sympathy.

Nevertheless, she was glad of Joe's presence as he accompanied her across the hall and along a musty passage to the glass-walled conservatory at the end. It was warmer at this western side of the house, and there was a lingering scent of citrus, although the trees that had borne the fruit had long since died.

If Patrick had known she was coming, he made a good attempt at not showing it. Perhaps he'd heard the footsteps and assumed it was just Joe, come to check if he was all right. Whatever, when they reached the doors into what had once been a hothouse he was sitting in an old canvas chair, gazing out at the shadows lengthening across the fields. The chair was placed so that his back was to them, and Isobel couldn't see any strapping across his shoulders.

'Hey, man.' Joe spoke first. 'You got a visitor.'

Patrick turned his head. Isobel didn't know what she had expected, but it certainly was not the sardonic look that crossed his face. 'Well, well, Isobel,' he said, making no attempt to get to his feet and greet her. 'So, the old lady went through with it after all.'

Isobel stiffened. 'If you mean your mother—'

'Of course I mean my mother,' snapped Patrick angrily. 'My God, she must have been more worried about her shares than I thought.'

'That's not true.' Isobel didn't believe that. 'Your mother cares about you.'

'Does she?' Patrick's tone was harsh. 'Well, at least she had more luck than I did. What did she say, for God's sake? What lies has she been telling? I tried my best, but you wouldn't listen to me!'

CHAPTER TWENTY

ISOBEL swallowed. 'She told me you'd been shot.'

Patrick's lips twisted. 'And you believed her?'

'Yes.' Isobel didn't quite know how to handle this, but when she looked for Joe's assistance she found he had melted away. 'Um—how are you? Are you all right?' She spread her hands helplessly. 'What are you doing here? I thought you were going to have this place renovated before you moved in.'

Patrick's mouth turned down. And then, as if realising he was being less than polite by remaining seated, he got somewhat stiffly to his feet. 'I think it was your mother who said that most people have to live in a property while they're having it redecorated. I decided to try it for myself.'

'But that's crazy!' The words burst from her.

'Why is it crazy? Joe and I are perfectly comfortable here, and I'm on the spot if anyone needs any advice.'

'But you don't have to,' protested Isobel frustratedly. 'And you're supposed to be recuperating!'

'Did my mother tell you that?' Isobel's silence was answer enough, and he forced a thin smile. 'Well, she's an old woman, and you know how old people love to fuss.'

'Patrick!'

The word exposed her anxiety, and, as if taking pity on her, he propped his hips on the stone sill that served as a base for the long windows. 'I'm all right,' he said flatly. Though now that Isobel could see his pale face she knew he wasn't. 'I told her I didn't want any sympathy from you.'

Isobel pressed her lips together. Was it her imagination or had he lost weight too? Certainly, the black jeans he was wearing seemed to hang rather loosely on his hips, and the sweatshirt was ideal for hiding his shape, its bulky folds disguising the bandages she knew must be underneath.

'Patrick, please,' she said, choosing her words carefully. 'Don't tell me now that you didn't want to see me unless you really want me to go away.'

His eyes darkened. 'When has it ever mattered to you what I want?'

'I suppose as long as it's mattered to you what I want,' she countered swiftly, and then took a moment to control her breathing. 'After—after that night we—we spent together, you made no attempt to see me again . . .'

'You mean I hadn't when you saw me in London.'

'Don't split hairs.' Isobel faced him bravely. 'You—you were dining with another woman! What was I supposed to think?'

'A woman I abandoned as soon as I saw you,' he reminded her grimly. 'A woman I haven't touched since that night we spent together.'

'And you expect me to believe that?'

'It's the truth, goddammit!' He winced as the strength of his emotions had him leaning almost aggressively towards her. 'All right, I admit it; I tried not to see you again.' His expression grew distant. 'I was afraid of the way you made me feel.'

Isobel swallowed. 'Of the way I made you feel?' she echoed. 'I don't—'

'Do I have to spell it out for you?' he demanded. 'I swore when Amanda left me that I'd never get seriously involved with another woman again. And I haven't.' He sighed. 'Oh, I'm not denying there have been other women. I'm not a monk, for God's sake. But they were all like Joanna. I provided a comfortable lifestyle and they provided—sex.'

Isobel linked her fingers together. 'Isn't that what I provided too?'

'No!' He almost came up off the stone sill, but the spasm of pain that crossed his face as he tried to do so held him back. 'Aren't you listening to what I'm saying? You were different.'

Isobel took a breath. 'Because I was a virgin?'

Patrick's expression grew derisive. 'Oh, yeah. You had to remind me of that, didn't you? It's not enough that you've taken my life and made a mockery of it; you have to turn the screw a little.'

'I didn't mean that.' Isobel took a step towards him. 'I want to believe you. I do. But I just don't understand why I—'

'Do you think I do?' he demanded, and her heart skipped a beat. Then, as if the effort was too much for him, he tipped his head back against the glass. 'Why did you come here, Belle? To gloat? It wasn't necessary. You've had your revenge a dozen times over.'

Isobel caught her lower lip between her teeth. 'I didn't come here for revenge.'

'Oh, no.' He tilted his head and looked at her. 'You came because my mother appealed to your sympathies. I forgot about that. Well, at least she achieved more than I did. She got you to speak to me.'

'If you'd told me—'

'What? That some poor mutt put a handful of buckshot into my shoulder? That would have done the trick?'

'Patrick...'

'What?' His eyes narrowed. 'I'm only telling it like it is. Isn't that what you always say?'

'Patrick—'

'For God's sake!' He turned his head away from her. 'What do you expect me to say? Thanks for coming, OK? See you around.'

Isobel closed her eyes for a moment. It was now or never, she thought fatalistically, and she knew that she'd never forgive herself if she left him now.

Licking her lips, she took another step forward. 'What you said,' she ventured, taking her courage in both hands and going with it. 'Did you really mean it?'

The sigh he uttered then was heartfelt. 'What I said when?' he asked wearily, turning to look at her again with obvious reluctance.

'The night—that night at your house,' she told him in an unsteady voice. 'When you said you—*loved* me.'

For a moment there was no perceptible change in Patrick's expression, but then an unwilling suspicion entered his eyes. 'Why?'

Isobel caught her breath. 'Will you answer the question?' she exclaimed fiercely. 'Did you mean it?'

'What is this? Isn't it enough to grind the poor bastard down? Do you have to put your heel on his neck too?'

'Patrick!'

'All right. I meant it.' His lips twisted. 'Of course I love you. What the hell do you think I've been telling you for the last fifteen minutes?'

Isobel felt the hot tears stinging behind her eyes. 'Oh, Patrick,' she whispered brokenly, and as if suddenly re-alising there might be another reason for her questions he rose from the stone sill, uncaring of the pain it obviously caused him.

'Belle?' he said huskily, and without another word she covered the space between them and wrapped her arms about his waist.

'You fool,' she said, sniffing back the tears as she buried her face against the reassuring warmth of his chest. 'Why didn't you make me believe you?'

'I tried to,' he said, and the catch in his voice reminded her that she was probably hurting him still.

But his arms came round her, and she knew that whatever happened in the future anything was worth the pure pleasure of being in his arms. She loved him; she might have fought against it, but she loved him. And whatever he wanted of her she would willingly give.

She could feel the strapping across his chest now, but when he got one hand under her chin and turned her face up to his she couldn't deny the hunger she'd been sup-pressing for so long. With a little groan, she cupped his cheek, and welcomed the urgent pressure of his mouth.

That her hunger was his hunger too was unmistakable. The kiss just went on and on, getting deeper and more des-perate by the second. Even the knowledge that he was not completely fit did nothing to temper their mood, and Isobel thought for a moment that he wouldn't be content until he'd made love to her there, on the dusty tiles.

But the pain of supporting her weight as well as his own eventually got the better of him, and although the oath he used wasn't pretty he had to set her back on her feet.

'Dammit,' he said, massaging his shoulder with frustrated fingers. 'God, I wish we were at the house.'

Isobel struggled to think sensibly. 'It's your own fault for martyring yourself by coming here,' she told him huskily, reluctant even now to let him go. 'What are you really doing here anyway? Apart from driving your mother crazy. They haven't even started renovating this place. No one lives without civil amenities these days.'

'I have civil amenities,' he told her drily. 'Well, there's water and electricity anyway. As for why I'm here, it was one way of being near you. Juvenile, I know, but I couldn't bear the sight of that house after you'd gone.'

'You're crazy!'

'Over you. Yes, I know.' The pain had subsided again, and as if aware of her needs he used his good arm to pull her closer. 'Which reminds me, I'm making all the running here. How about you?'

Isobel's lips quivered. 'You know I love you.'

'Do I?'

'You should.' She permitted herself a quick glance up at him. 'I wouldn't be here otherwise.'

'Oh, I don't know.' He was being deliberately obtuse. 'You could just have taken pity on me and—'

'I love you,' said Isobel fiercely. 'You know I do.' She took a breath. 'And—and we could always go to my house.'

Patrick's lips twitched. 'I thought that was sacrosanct,' he teased, and she remembered in time to pull the punch she was tempted to deliver to his midriff.

'It was until you came along,' she retorted, but her eyes were dancing now. 'Do you think Joe would mind booking into a hotel?'

Patrick laughed. 'I'd say he'd be everlastingly grateful. I'm sure it was he who persuaded my mother to interfere.'

'Thank God she did.'

'Amen to that,' agreed Patrick softly. 'Oh, Belle, you'll never regret this. I promise you that.'

It was dark when Isobel woke up, and for a moment she felt disorientated. It was the knowledge that there was someone in bed with her that felt so strange. But then she remembered what had happened, and a feeling of exhilaration swept over her. It was Patrick who was sharing her bed, Patrick who would be sharing her life from now on.

Or not?

The awareness that she hadn't yet been completely honest with him caused her some misgivings. What place did someone like her have in his sophisticated scheme of things? It was all very well imagining their life together as one of pleasure and fulfilment. But without any real commitment was it fair?

She ran an exploring hand across her flat stomach. If there had been only herself to think about, the question wouldn't even have arisen. But how would Patrick react to being told the truth? Would he believe her when she said she hadn't lied to him? How long could she keep her secret before he guessed?

The feeling of well-being she had been nurturing fled, and in its place she felt the first twinges of despair. How could she let him go, when she knew her life depended on his being in it? How could she start again after tonight?

She started when another hand came to join hers on her stomach and then slid down with thrilling possession between her legs. 'Are you awake?' Patrick murmured, moving to bury his face in the hollow of her shoulder. 'Don't mind me,' he added, caressing the inner curve of her thigh. 'I just wanted to assure myself it wasn't a dream.'

'It wasn't a dream,' Isobel told him a little breathlessly. However weary Patrick had been before they'd reached the cottage, he'd been hotly awake when he'd tumbled her into bed. And, for all that there must have been times when his shoulder had pained him, he hadn't shown it, making love to her with all the urgency and hunger she could have wished for.

'That's good,' he said softly, reaching across her and using his uninjured arm to switch on the lamp. 'What time is it? Heavens—no wonder I'm hungry. I don't remember the last time I had a meal.'

Isobel blinked up at him. 'Didn't you have any lunch?'

'No.' Patrick bent his head and bit her lower lip. 'Oh, Joe got some fish and chips, but I didn't want any. I haven't been very hungry lately. Well—' his tongue brushed along her teeth '—not for food.'

'Pat!'

'What?' He rubbed her nose with his. 'I can do with losing some weight.'

'You can't.' She touched his midriff, and then let her hand trail lower. 'A man should always eat to keep his strength up.'

'To keep his what up?' Patrick exclaimed half-laughingly, the words ending in a gulp when her hand closed about him. 'God, Belle, I'm supposed to be convalescing, you know that.'

'Do you mind?'

The words were provocative, but he sensed the shy uncertainty she was feeling, and, covering her hand with his, he shook his head. 'So long as you don't mind taking the consequences,' he told her thickly. 'Hell, I wasn't all that hungry anyway.'

This time when his body slid slickly into hers she was ready for him, arching up to him and winding her legs about his hips. 'I love you,' she said as he bent to capture her mouth, and his response was everything she could have wanted and more.

But when the tremors had stopped racking her body, and Patrick was no longer shaking in her arms, she knew she couldn't delay the inevitable for very much longer. He had to know; he deserved to know—whatever that might do to their relationship.

Yet she also knew that she couldn't tell him here, not in this place where she had known such misery and such ecstasy. So, despite the fact that he protested when she moved away from him, she slid off the bed and, gathering up her silk kimono, slipped her arms into the sleeves.

'Hey, that suits you,' he said, his eyes still dark and glazed with passion. 'Do you want to get back in again?'

'I—no—not yet,' she mumbled, heading for the door. 'I thought as you were hungry I might make you a sandwich.'

'Are you bringing it back here?'

'Um—no.' She paused in the doorway. 'Perhaps you should come downstairs.'

His brows drew together. 'That sounds ominous.' He pushed himself up on one elbow. 'You're not about to tell me this was just a brief remission, are you?'

'No.' A trace of colour entered her cheeks. 'No, of course not.'

'Good.' He swung his legs out of the bed, apparently uncaring that he was stark naked. 'Because I wouldn't like to have another relapse.'

Isobel managed a small smile. 'Have I said anything to make you think that?'

'No.' He regarded her consideringly. 'But I'm not used to having someone make sandwiches for me who isn't being paid for the privilege.' He grinned a heart-stopping grin. 'Promise me you'll do this sometimes, even after we're married, hmm?'

As he was reaching for his trousers, he heard her indrawn breath. 'Married?' she whispered. 'I thought you said you'd never get married again.'

He pushed one leg into his trousers, and then fixed her with a wry look. 'I also said I'd never get seriously involved with a woman again,' he reminded her drily. 'And if you think I'm going to risk you walking out on me again—'

'Oh, Pat!'

Her cry was so tremulous that he hurriedly pushed his other leg into the trousers and got to his feet, crossing the space between them in a couple of strides.

'What?' he asked as she burrowed against him. 'What is it? God, surely you knew I was going to ask you to marry me?'

'How could I?' she mumbled.

'OK,' he said soothingly. 'OK, you couldn't know. But here it is, for what it's worth. Will you marry me? Please?'

Isobel couldn't speak. She could only move her head in an affirmative gesture, and he put his fingers beneath her chin and turned her face up to his.

'What's wrong?' he asked, his concern deepening as he saw her tear-wet cheeks. His thumb brushed a drop from the end of her nose. 'Don't you want to?'

'Of course I do,' she got out at last. 'But there's something—something I haven't told you.'

His brows drew together. 'You're not already married?' His tone mixed doubtful humour and uncertainty in equal measures.

'No.' She sniffed. 'Of course not.' She took a deep breath. 'I'm—pregnant.'

Patrick put his hands on her shoulders. 'You're *what*?'

She couldn't meet his eyes. 'You heard me.'

'Do you mean to tell me that when you said you weren't—?'

'No.' Isobel sighed. 'I really didn't know then.'

Patrick stared at her for a long minute, and then shook his head. 'How long have you known?'

'Just a few days.'

'But it's been several weeks since—'

'I know.' Isobel moved her shoulders in a helpless gesture. 'I know it's hard to believe, but it never occurred to me that—well, that I really might be.'

'Rough justice,' said Patrick drily, releasing her to run distracted fingers through his hair. He half turned away from her and took a steadying breath. 'So what do you want me to do? Naturally, I'll take responsibility for everything . . .'

'What are you talking about?' Isobel caught his arm and, uncaring that she might be hurting him, swung him round to face her. 'I want you to marry me, of course. Isn't that what you want too?'

'Not if you're only marrying me because you're expecting my baby.'

Isobel caught her breath. 'You're crazy! Do you know that? You're crazy, Pat. It's nearly the twenty-first century, and you're suggesting that I'd marry you just to get a father for my baby?'

His eyes darkened. 'Then why didn't you tell me?'

'Because I didn't want you to—to want me just because I was pregnant!' she exclaimed frustratedly. 'I tried that once, remember? I wanted you to want me for myself.'

Patrick frowned. 'Well, you know I do,' he said harshly.

'And you don't mind?'

'Mind?' Now it was his turn to look perplexed.

'Well, that we're going to start our married life as—as parents.'

Patrick's face cleared, and he pulled her convulsively against him, his hands sliding beneath the thin kimono. 'Does this feel as if I mind?' he demanded thickly, crushing her to him. 'God, Belle, I can't believe it. When I woke up this morning, I thought I had nothing; now I have everything.'

'Me too,' she breathed, sliding her arms about his neck.

'I knew it was a good idea to buy Foxworth,' he said huskily. 'The country air is much better for children than the town. And I can always commute. I've been thinking of getting a helicopter for my own use.'

Isobel shook her head. 'The baby will be born before that place is finished,' she protested.

'Not if I have anything to do with it,' he assured her. 'And meanwhile we'll commute between here and Lauriston Square.'

'We?'

'Of course. I have no intention of leaving my wife behind.'

'What about Caprice?'

'I'm sure Chris can handle it for the time being. After we move into Foxworth, it's up to you.'

'You mean you won't object if I want to go back to work?'

'Hey, this is nearly the twenty-first century,' said Patrick slyly. 'I wouldn't dream of telling such an independent woman what to do!'

HARLEQUIN  PRESENTS®

Men who find their way to fatherhood by fair means, by foul, or even by default!

Coming next month:
Single dad requires protection!
in

#1879 LOOKING AFTER DAD
by
Elizabeth Oldfield

Before Jess knows it, Lorcan Hunter has offered her a permanent assignment to be personal bodyguard to him and his little girl—for life!

Available in April wherever
Harlequin books are sold.

Look us up on-line at: http://www.romance.net

FHTP4

HARLEQUIN  PRESENTS®

She couldn't let him touch her!

Coming next month:

#1873 A DAUGHTER'S DILEMMA
by
Miranda Lee

Vaughan Slater wanted Caroline more than any
woman he'd ever known. So did that mean he would
seduce her, make love to her and then walk away?
Like Carolyn knew he had, ten years before?

Available in April wherever
Harlequin books are sold.

Look us up on-line at: http://www.romance.net

FORB4

Happy Birthday to

Harlequin Romance®

It's party time....
This year is our
40th anniversary!

**Forty years of
bringing you the best
in romance fiction—and
the best just keeps
getting better!**

To celebrate, we're planning
three months of fun, and prizes.

Not to mention, of course,
some fabulous books...

The party starts in **April** with:

Betty Neels
Emma Richmond
Kate Denton
Barbara McMahon

Come join the party!

Available wherever Harlequin books are sold.   HR40THG1